THIS IS

THE STORY
OF NICK.

C.A. JULAL

To the hero inside all of us.

1

THE STORY OF BEGINNINGS

To those who knew him, he may have seemed peculiar. However, his apparent oddness was ironically attributed to the fact that he was ordinary to a fault. Save a nose that was slightly crooked, there was nothing distinguishable about him. He was as plain as they come. He was also pragmatic. Even the slightest disorder left him troubled. For instance, there were always precisely eleven spoons and eleven forks in his kitchen drawer at all times   nothing more and nothing less. If even one spoon or fork were missing, he would search frantically until it was found. To an observer, his life would have seemed formulaic, but one could argue that all lives are formulaic, his was simply specific.

He woke up every morning at precisely 7:00 AM, leaving ample time to sip tea and peruse the morning paper. He never actually read any articles. He simply enjoyed reading the headlines, as they made him feel as if he was in some way contributing to world affairs. By 8:00 am he would leave his duplex, which was much too small to be considered a home, but always seemed quite too large for one person. He would walk with pace and purpose to work, never once stopping to smell the roses — which he did not like anyway as he felt roses represented unfair idealistic notions of love.

He arrived at work every day at 8:30 AM. Thirty minutes earlier than necessary. This was partly due to the fact that he had an innate need to be punctual, but mostly because Sam, the receptionist, was in his mind, the woman of his dreams. While it would be a stretch to even call these two acquaintances, since no more than a few words were ever exchanged between them, that small detail did not derail his fantasies.

Once at work, he would take the stairs to the second floor where he worked in the IT department. Although he could have just as easily have taken the elevator, he felt that a single floor did not warrant the time spent in such a confined space. His work was not interesting in the slightest. Most of the queries he dealt with could be solved within minutes, but due to the fact that people often assume they are experts, most of his time was spent convincing others to listen to his technical advice.

After work, he would gather his belongings and rush out the door. He did not care to bid good-bye to any of his coworkers, because to him, work was no place to make friends. His only delay upon leaving was to see if Sam was still around. Once again, he never spoke to her. He just imagined a world in which he did.

Upon arriving at his rickety duplex, he would change out of his work clothes, prepare another cup of tea and mindlessly stare at the television. Oftentimes, he would watch the same shows over and over again, too afraid to take a chance on something new. Despite his apathy, he did, occasionally associate with people. Every Tuesday and Sunday, he would visit his sister, Kate and her two children — Anthony and Allison. He felt that it was his duty to support them, despite the fact that he had no idea how to identify with children.

On Saturdays (and other random encounters), he spent time with his good friend, Tom. Tom was his antithesis. If someone were to ask him to describe Tom, he would simply reply with two words: blubbering fool. That being said, he had known Tom his entire life, and to abandon such a friendship would be like abandoning everything he knew. And so, just like the television shows, Tom continued to be an integral part of his life.

As you can see, there was nothing interesting about this man. His life was like clockwork, and his demeanor was uninspiring. He was arguably the most uninteresting person one could ever meet. But, even the plainest of folk have a story, and this is his.

This is the story of Nick.

2

THE STORY OF A GOOD DAY

Missing Child in the Metro Area.

Nick sipped his tea as he read the headline over and over. He could not help but feel sorry for the child. Someone should do something about it. But with the turn of the page, his feelings subsided as quickly as they had arrived. It was easy for him to detach from stories. After all, he only ever read headlines. He could not trouble himself with the entire story, especially when headlines so nicely summed up the points for him. A child was missing, whether it was a boy or a girl, older or younger, it did not matter. All he needed to know was right there in front of him.

Nick glanced at his watch – a gift given to him by his childhood friend when he was a teenager. He still had five minutes to spare, but he believed an early start might mean an early finish. He got up from his chair and quickly washed the dishes. He could not bother with dish washers, as they were too slow and unreliable for his liking. It took him three minutes to finish his chores. As he walked out the door to face the beauty of the shining sun, and the sounds of the world around him, he quickly put on his shades and earphones to negate the irritation. While his shades were a luxury, his earphones were a necessity. He could not stand hearing anything but the music of his choosing. Any other sounds were simply noise.

Nick strolled down the street keeping his head up, bobbing awkwardly to the sounds of The Jackson 5 classic, *Blame It On The Boogie*. Nick did not drive. Not for environmental or financial reasons, but simply because he felt his feet were an adequate means of transportation. A vehicle requires maintenance, experience, and a desire to show off. Similar to relationships, Nick could not be bothered with any of it.

The music blared in his ears drowning out the sounds from the outside world. Nick was not fond of the real world as he found it to be rather boring for his liking. He preferred to imagine a more pleasant world; one in which the birds chirped and the wind whistled. In that moment, nothing else mattered to Nick. Ironically, if Nick had in fact just taken off his headphones, he would have realized that birds were chirping and the wind was whistling. However, none of it mattered, because Nick's daydreams were his, and his alone, and nothing else could ever compare.

After his long daydream, Nick arrived at his place of work — a computer company that dealt with everything from hardware to software. Nick worked in the IT department, and his only job was to make sure that the servers were in good working order. Nick was particularly grateful for the fact that this company had the best equipment available, because it meant that the servers almost never went down.

As he walked into the building, he paused for a moment in the main lobby to see Sam — the apple of his eye, his heart's desire, his one true... like. Love was a mystery to him, and if he could ever solve it, he was sure that she would be the answer. Slowly, he walked towards her desk, and removed his headphones. Surely a woman of this quality deserved his full, undivided attention.

"Good morning, wonderful," greeted Nick.

"Oh, Nick, you always know how to make a woman blush. How have you been?" replied Sam.

"Oh, not as good as you."

"Stop it, people are going think we are having an affair," giggled Sam.

"Well imagine what they are going to think when we run away together."

"Oh, it's like music to my ears. Take me away."

"Okay, we'll leave tonight. We'll fly to Tuscany, eat nothing but bread, and drink wine until we can no longer stand."

"Oh, if only it was all real."

"Hey... someday, it might be."

It had all felt so real, until he realized that an older woman was staring at him with what looked like deep concern. "I love this song. Sometimes I get carried away," said Nick, shrugging his shoulders. She did not reply, but shook her head and darted in another direction. Nick continued to stare as the woman trudged off into the distance. His daydreaming was both a gift and a curse. While he loved it, it also quite often left him exposed and in constant need of an explanation.

As he continued to contemplate the scenarios he concocted, a swift glance toward Sam was enough to break his contemplative stance. Nick was confident that today would be the day that he made progress with her. To Nick, their relationship was inevitable. He was sure they shared many interests and commonalities – an integral aspect of any budding relationship. For instance, they both worked at the same place. That may not seem like much; but of the many countries, cities, and places to work, Sam had chosen to be a receptionist at this particular place of business. That alone was something. On top of that, Nick enjoyed music and television. While Sam had never given any indication of liking either, he was sure that she liked at least one of them.

Nick readjusted the strap on his bag, and strode towards the reception desk. Even if he did not speak with Sam, the stairs to his floor were right beside the desk, giving him a quick and easy retreat. That was the thing about Nick, he always had an escape plan.

As Nick neared the desk, Sam looked up and gave him a courteous smile.

"Hey Kevin, may I help you with anything?"

Nick stared blankly, embarrassed that she had forgotten his name. He could correct her, but feared that doing so would put a strain on a possibly scintillating conversation.

"I am well, and you?" said Nick eagerly.

"I'm well, but I asked if you needed help."

Nick began to scramble for a response. It was clear that this conversation was going nowhere. The first indication of that should have been the fact the she did not even know his real name. However, Nick thought that perhaps a little banter about local affairs might turn things around.

"I'm missing a child."

"What? You lost your child? Did you call the authorities?!" Shouted Sam, as she picked up her phone.

"No, sorry, not my child, there is a child missing in... the world... in general."

"Do you know the child?" asked Sam.

"No... well, I saw a picture, but no, I don't." stated Nick, confused on where he was going with this.

"Okay, how am I supposed to help you?"

"You... you can't, I guess. I just thought you ought to know."

"Well, thanks for spreading the message, Kevin."

Just as the conversation seemed to be coming to an end, Andy, a co-worker in the IT department came strolling by. "Hey Nick, excited for a new day in the office?" asked Andy, punching Nick's shoulders.

"Not now, Andy! Just go upstairs and we'll talk later," said Nick.

"This guy," said Andy, pointing at Nick. "You always crack me up. Andy scampered off toward the elevator, leaving Nick and Sam to continue their awkward stare down.

Unsure of what to say, Nick placed his hands in his pocket, gave a tight-lip smile and shrugged his shoulders. To him, this may have seemed like a friendly shrug, but the gesture was in fact both terrifying and deeply concerning.

"I thought your name was Kevin?" asked Sam, looking even more confused.

"Did you say Kevin? Oh, I thought you said Nick. They sound so much alike."

"No, they really don't."

"They kind of do. NIIII-IIICK... KEVVVVVV-IIIN... see?" emphasized Nick, struggling to find a way to similarly pronounce two very dissimilar names.

It was clear by the look on her face that Sam was both uninterested and unimpressed.

"Who's Kevin then?" asked Sam.

"Kevin works in legal."

"And you work in...?"

"I work in the IT department."

"Okay... Nick from the IT department, good... talking with you," responded Sam hesitantly.

Nick stared for a moment, unsure of whether the conversation was coming to an end, or if Sam was merely making a declarative comment about the overall quality of the conversation. After careful consideration, Nick deemed the former to be true; not because he believed the conversation needed to end, but simply because he could not think of anything interesting to say.

"Well, good day, milady," Nick said while bowing in a courteous manner. And with that, Nick strutted confidently toward the stairs

"That went rather well," Nick mumbled, as he climbed the staircase. Nick had indeed made progress with Sam. It was as a matter of fact, their longest conversation.

The previous title holder belonged to:

How do you do? asked Nick.
I am well, and yourself? replied Sam.
Ha-ha — Hilarious. said Nick.

THIS IS THE STORY OF NICK.

Okay... said Sam.

Nick reached his desk and plopped himself comfortably in his swivel chair. While he did not love his job, there was something relaxing about his desk. When Nick sat at his desk, he felt important. Regardless of the fact that Nick spent most of the time playing solitaire and monitoring screens — to Nick, these were the rewards for being the best at his job. In the ten years that Nick had worked at this job, the servers had never gone down. He was Mr. Reliable — a hero to his coworkers. As Nick basked in the thought of his heroism, he was rudely awoken by his annoying co-worker, Andy.

"So, I saw you talking to Sam. How did it go?" asked Andy inquisitively.

"Andy, you really have no tact. I just had a pleasant conversation with a beautiful woman, and you have the nerve to gossip about it."

"I am so sorry... I really am."

"It's okay. If you must know, I think she has taken a liking to me," said Nick boastfully.

"Really? Are you going to ask her out?"

"You act like you're surprised that I can get a woman like her. And to answer your question, no. It all takes time, Andy."

"You're right. I am so happy for you. If you guys get married, can I be the best man?" pleaded Andy.

"No, but if you like, I will let you be a server at my wedding."

"That sounds... amazing! Thank you."

Nick really did not like Andy. There was no particular reason for it either. Andy had always been nothing but kind and courteous toward him. Nick thought that perhaps it was his incessant desire to please others. Regardless, Nick found him to be a great annoyance, and often found humor in belittling him.

"Any issues we need to fix today, Andy?" questioned Nick.

"I've got them all taken care of except one," replied Andy, handing him the ticket.

Nick read the issue very carefully, making sure not to miss any details. It did not take him long to realize the problem. Nick picked up his phone and dialed the number on the ticket.

"Good morning, ma'am. This is Nick from the IT department. You said that you were having trouble with your computer."

"Yes, I pressed the power button, but nothing seems to work," replied the woman in a panic.

"Not to worry. This is a very common issue. May I ask... have you plugged in the computer?"

"Yes... of course it's plugged."

"Well then, perhaps you need to click the power button," said Nick, barely masking his arrogance.

"I've clicked it about a thousand times," insisted the woman.

"Well, a thousand and one might do the trick."

"Just to make sure, which is the power button again?"

"It's the really big one at the very front of the computer."

"I am literally clicking it as we speak," groaned the woman."

"Ma'am, you do know that the monitor, or the screen if you will, is not the computer. The computer is below the screen," said Nick, spinning his chair in semicircles.

"Ah, it started working again. Thank you. These things always give trouble" said the woman, embarrassed that she had been clicking the wrong button.

"You're very welcome. Have a great day," said Nick. As the phone clicked off, Nick felt a sense of relief to be done with the issue. "What an idiot," mumbled Nick, just loud enough for Andy to grin and mouth the word *sorry*.

It did not take much for Nick to become annoyed. The fact that he was forced to have a conversation and help incompetent people seemed like a cruel and torturous fate. Nick opened his solitaire app, and began to shuffle the cards. He did not actually like playing solitaire, but enjoyed the sound the cards made when he clicked shuffle. While others may use yoga and exercise as a means of mediation and relaxation, the sound of computerized cards was all Nick ever needed.

He continued this loop for the next hour until he decided that it was time to take a break. He opened his lunch bag, and there sat a roast beef sandwich on rye. For the past ten years, Nick had had the exact same lunch, and never once had he complained. In fact, it was often one of the highlights of his day. Foregoing his lunch would be catastrophic to the ritual that he had created, and doing so seemed blasphemous. He could not imagine the hellish ordeal that might unfold if for some reason he did not have his roast beef sandwich.

The rest of Nick's day consisted of shuffling, complaining, and shuffling some more. It was a routine, but Nick rather enjoyed it. On some strange level, it gave him comfort and purpose. He knew what to expect and what was expected from him, and that very notion shaped his entire identity.

As soon as the clock hit 5:00pm, Nick gathered his belongings and bolted out the door. As he headed toward the stairs, it did not cross his mind to say goodbye to Andy. Nick hated saying goodbye, simply out of sheer awkwardness. Whenever leaving anywhere, he always preferred a quiet escape rather than having to deal with a formal departure.

Nick entered the lobby and saw Sam reading something at her desk. He imagined her looking up and smiling   waving him down to come talk. Just as the fantasy entered his mind, it transitioned into another one. This time he was in an all-black suit and she was in a beautiful, flowing red dress. He gave her his hand and she grasped it almost immediately. Without a word, the two of them began to dance and sway, looking wistfully into each other's eyes.

Nick opened his eyes only to see Sam staring at him strangely. His fantasy had escaped his thoughts and taken form within his reality. However, Sam was not dancing or waving him down. The only person dancing was him. Nick quickly regained his composure, smiled awkwardly and strode out the door. As awkward as this encounter may have been, Nick was simply glad that she had even noticed him, and that was more than he could have asked for.

Nick arrived at his home in a hurry. It was a Tuesday, and he was expected to have dinner at his sister's place. He would not be long inside his home, he simply needed to drop off things from work and he would be right back out the door. As he entered the foyer, he heard a strange sound. Someone was inside.

He crept quietly toward the kitchen – the sound becoming louder and louder. All he could hear was the rustling of utensils and the groaning of what sounded like a man – or a very deep-voiced woman.

"Hello?" shouted Nick, "If you are planning on robbing me, please do it quickly because I am rather busy, and I would prefer not to be stabbed."

"Relax, Nick. I just came to eat some food," responded the voice.

"Tom?" said Nick, as he walked into the kitchen to confront him. "What the hell are you doing?" As Nick looked up, he saw the tall, lean frame of his friend eating a sandwich.

"I just told you, I'm hungry."

"How the hell did you get in?"

"I have a key," said Tom with his mouth full, holding up a key.

"I never gave you a key!"

"I know. I had one made," replied Tom nonchalantly.

"You scare me," said Nick, shaking his head in disbelief.

"People always say that.," Tom shrugged. "I don't really get it."

"Listen, I can't really stay, I have to go visit Kate and the kids," stated Nick.

"Oh, that sounds like fun. Can I come?"

"No, you can't. She hates you."

"See, I don't get that. What have I ever done to her?"

"You tried to sell her house," said Nick.

"I was doing her a favour," scoffed Tom.

"She was still living in it," said Nick in disbelief. "You also used her children to help you sell merchandise at that booth in the mall."

"Hey, I was trying to teach them the value of hard work. Sorry for trying to instill valuable life lessons."

"You had them selling bootleg phones while you played videogames at my place."

"They need to be independent!" shouted Tom

"They're children! Anthony isn't even ten years old yet."

"Okay, I get it. She doesn't like me. Whatever... I just came to tell you about my new job."

"What is it?" asked Nick.

"I'm selling soap door-to-door."

"Soap? That's your new job? Why would you think that would work?"

"The soap business is very lucrative. Everyone needs soap, and I am willing to sell it to you right at your door," said Tom, as if he was trying to sell the idea to Nick.

It seemed that Tom had a new business venture every week, as none of his ideas ever seemed to succeed — at least not in Nick's eyes. His previous venture had been a go-kart business targeted towards people of a smaller stature. Tom had called it: *Little Cars 4 Little People.* If Nick was honest with himself, he was surprised that the idea had lasted as long as it had.

"What happened to the go-kart business?"

"Apparently, little people take offense to people trying to sell them little cars. Here I thought I was being a humanitarian," said Tom, shaking his head.

Nick pondered the thought of how Tom actually went about selling go-karts to little people. Did he show up at their door like he did with soap? Or did he spot them along the road walking and think, hey, you could use a ride. Nick's mind jumped from idea to idea until he remembered that he was due for dinner at his sister's place. "Listen, I need to head to Kate's. Could you give me a lift?"

"Just using me for rides," responded Tom.

It did not bother Tom to drive. In fact, he quite enjoyed driving, but to be asked to do a favour, regardless of how small, irked him beyond belief. This was something that Nick knew all too well. Nevertheless, Nick needed a ride, and that easily trumped any fear of getting Tom upset.

"Well, seeing as you apparently use my food, my home, and my money, the least you can do is drop me off at my sisters. It's on your way, for God's sake," said Nick, becoming more and more infuriated with his friend.

"Alright. I'll take you. Calm down."

"Thank you," said Nick, as his emotions began to level.

"Do you mind pitching in for gas though? I just could use..."

"I am not going to even respond to you," said Nick, as he stormed out the door.

"Ha-ha – actually that is a response. So, it looks like you're wrong there," said Tom, following Nick out of the house and into his car – a beat-up, old Honda that had clearly seen better days.

The two barely spoke on the way to Kate's place. This had nothing to do with their little spat earlier. In truth, a lack of conversation was a common occurrence. The silence was simply due to the fact that sitting in a car with only one other person is an awkward affair – regardless of the relationship. To Nick, the very idea of being trapped in a confined space with any individual was a horrible ordeal.

Upon arriving at Kate's place, Nick offered an awkward farewell to Tom, before giving him some money and shutting the door. He jogged lightly toward the home – a small, old semi, similar in size to Nick's duplex. How a family of three could live in such conditions was beyond him.

Nick rang the doorbell and was no sooner greeted by his nephew and niece.

"Uncle Nick, you're here!" shouted Allison, as she jumped on him with both arms wrapped around his slender frame.

"I come every Tuesday and Sunday. I thought you two would be used to it by now," said Nick, trying to pry his niece's fingers off of him.

"Allison, get off uncle, you're hurting him," said Anthony.

"Your brother is right, get off. Let me at least come inside."

Allison removed her vice-like grip and let Nick come in. However, as Nick stepped through the door, he was once again immediately greeted with tight hugs – this time by both Anthony and Allison.

"Anthony, you just told your sister to get off of me, and now you're doing the same thing?" said Nick, struggling to breathe.

"At least I waited for you to actually come inside," responded Anthony.

As Nick stood awkwardly, hoping that his lovable niece and nephew would finally find something else to occupy their attention,

Kate came into the room. "Nick, I am so glad you're here," said Kate, joining her children in a very awkward hug.

"Not you, too," sighed Nick, squinting his eyes as if he were in the most unbearable pain. "Why are you all so touchy-feely? What happened to a good old-fashioned nod?"

"Don't pretend you don't love it," said Kate, finally releasing her grip.

"I am not pretending," said Nick, as Kate glared at him and smirked.

"Come in, dinner is ready," said Allison, pulling her uncle's hand toward the dining room.

Nick quietly followed and took his seat opposite his sister, with both children taking a seat on either side of him. As he made himself comfortable, Nick was greeted with a plate of tilapia, with rice and mixed-vegetables. Nick was particularly excited, not because he liked fish, but because eating dinner at someone's home meant that Nick did not have to clean anything   and that was the way Nick liked things. Twice a week, Nick's sister would prepare a meal for him in hopes that he would come over and spend time. Nick always obliged. He often found his interactions with his niece and nephew to be awkward, but he rather enjoyed his time with his sister.

Nick did not waste any time digging into his meal, and devouring the contents of his plate with great speed and efficiency. At this point, Kate was used to his eating habits, but his niece and nephew still stared in amazement.

"Uncle Nick," said Anthony, breaking his gaze away from his uncle's plate. "Heard of anything new?"

Nick quickly swallowed his food as he pondered the question. He was unsure of how to answer. Of course there were many things new that he had heard, but what would interest a child of ten? "Hmmm... well, there is a missing child," said Nick, returning his attention back toward his plate.

"You're missing a child?" said Allison, with a look of worry in her eyes.

"No. Why does everyone think that? There is a child missing in the world... in this city actually," said Nick.

"Nick! Is this appropriate for children to hear?" questioned Kate,

15

looking at him sternly.

"I rather think so," Nick piped back.

Nick could not understand why his sister had protested so vehemently against the conversation. He felt strongly that children these days knew very little about current affairs. If anything, his sister should have been thanking him for educating her children. God only knows what they were learning in school. It was about time that someone spoke the truth, Nick thought as he gazed at his fish, wishing that it was something a little heavier, like a steak or even a pork-chop.

"Was it a kid like us?" asked Anthony.

"Actually, a lot like you," replied Nick.

"Nick, please," protested Kate.

"Will we go missing?" whimpered Allison.

"Quite possibly," shot-back Nick.

"Nick!" yelled Kate.

"I am just saying, we shouldn't rule out the possibility. That would just be careless," said Nick very casually.

"Children, why don't you wash up and play some games, we'll discuss this stuff later, okay?" said Kate empathetically.

"So we're not going to go missing?" asked Anthony.

"No. You are both safe here with me... and believe it or not, with your uncle." said Kate, as she got up and hugged both of them before sending them off to wash up.

"Again with the hugging," said Nick.

"Maybe if you were hugged more often, you wouldn't be so cold," smirked Kate, shaking her head.

Nick simply smiled at his sister and then solemnly gazed at the ground below him.

"What's the matter?" asked Kate.

Nick continued his gaze, unsure whether he wanted to look up, or if he even could.

"Nick?" Kate called out once more.

"When you said that I needed to be hugged more often, the only thing I could think about was, when was the last time you were hugged by someone?"

"Anthony and Allison shower me with hugs every day," replied

Kate.

"No, I mean..."

"I know what you mean. It's been almost five years since Ron passed away, but when he was alive, he hugged me every day. And on top of that, he gave me two wonderful children."

Nick smiled as his sister reminisced of her late husband. Sure, he masked his intentions of his visits with a need for food and an obligation to be somewhat social, but the truth was, he visited her just to make sure that she was still okay.

"You know, when I lost my husband, you also lost your best-friend," Kate added.

Nick found it difficult to swallow. Hearing such words aloud was not something Nick was used to. "I still have Tom," said Nick with a half-hearted laugh.

"Tom is an idiot, and you know Ron didn't like him either," said Kate, as she rolled her eyes.

"Yeah, I suppose Tom is a bit of an idiot."

"A bit? Nick, you give him way more credit than he deserves," responded Kate.

Nick chuckled at his sister's fervent stance on his friend. Tom was a fool. Nick could not deny this. However, he was the only real friend he had left. Nick thought about Ron and the memories the two childhood friends shared. He glanced toward his watch, and could not help but feel a pang in his chest.

"Kate, thank you for dinner, but it's getting late. I'd best be off."

"Of course, Nick. Thank you for coming. She hugged him tightly. Despite his constant protests against hugs, Nick did not say anything this time. While he did not hug her back   as it was against his very beliefs   he did not pull away either. He stood perfectly still as his sister bid him farewell.

Nick walked home in a hurry, eagerly awaiting the comfort of his bed. He hated being out late on a work night, and 8:30pm was far too late for his liking. Upon arriving home, he quickly washed up, got into bed, turned the television and fell asleep to the sound of the news.

To Nick, this was a good day. While there may have been a few awkward moments, and bumps on the road, they were harmless inconveniences to which Nick was more than capable of dealing with. Nonetheless, while some days may be ordinarily good, others are extraordinarily bad.

3

THE STORY OF
A NOT SO GOOD DAY

Nick's eyes fluttered as the morning light crept into his room. Realizing that a new day had begun, an unfamiliar smile stretched across his face. Nick felt rested. It was a strange feeling, as he usually awoke with a yearning for more sleep. Upon realizing the oddity, Nick awoke in a hurry, grabbing his phone quickly and somewhat anxiously. The time read 8:30am   he was late. In his ten years of working, Nick had never been late. He was perpetually early for everything. The very idea of being late had never so much as crossed his mind, let alone become a reality.

Nick scrambled to get out of bed and get ready. He threw on clothes, not taking a second look to consider what he was even putting on. While keeping a professional appearance was important to him, the thought of not being able to read the paper and relax before heading out infuriated him. He rushed down the stairs and stood between the door and his kitchen. Nick was at a crossroads. He desperately needed his morning tea, but doing so would surely ensure his tardiness. Nick had to choose between his punctuality and his tea — a dilemma for the ages. As he stood motionless, contemplating his choices, an idea sprung from desperation.

Nick pulled out his phone and dialed Tom's number. Tom had a car, and Nick knew Tom had nothing to do — save selling soap door-to-door. As the phone rang, Nick paced frantically across his tiny hall. There was no answer — of course. Tom always seemed to be around except when you actually needed him.

There was no time to be pissed at Tom. Nick was late, and he needed to leave. He threw on the first pair of sneakers he found and bolted out the door. However, his determination was short-lived, as he tripped and fell mere meters away from his front door. Nick had forgotten that this particular pair of sneakers was horrible. The shoe never fit quite right, and the laces always seemed to come undone. Realizing that changing shoes would consume even more time, Nick decided to carry on, galloping in an awkward fashion in order to prevent himself from tripping again.

His gallop to work was not enjoyable. He had forgotten to take his headphones with him, so there was no music to accompany him on his journey. To Nick's dismay, he was forced to hear the world around him, and on this particular day, there happened to be construction — the bane of... well... everyone.

Nick reached the lobby of his office building at precisely 9:05am. While it was highly unlikely that anyone would say anything, or even notice, this fact bothered Nick tremendously. His reliable, punctual persona had vanished in a single day. Nick continued his gallop toward the stairs, ignoring his desire to fanaticize about Sam, who was far too preoccupied with her fashion magazine, anyway.

As he traversed the stairway and reached his floor, he was instantly greeted by his bumbling co-worker, Andy.

"Nick, thank God you're here! Where have you been, bitch?" Andy was breathing heavily — not that Nick cared.

"You call me a bitch one more time and I'll slap you, and then I'll go to your house and slap your mother Clara. That's how serious I am," replied Nick.

"That's not my mother's name, but that is beside the point. I'm sorry, I was trying to be funny... which I shouldn't have because you're late..."

Nick froze instantly. Of all people, Andy had called him out on his tardiness. To be late is one thing, to have Andy mention it was just downright deplorable. Nick frantically thought of an excuse that could not only redeem him, but allow him to regain respect and authority over his co-worker.

"Andy, if you must know, the reason I am late is because I had to rescue a cat from a tree," said Nick authoritatively.

"Really? That's incredible. You're a real hero."

Nick chuckled politely, downplaying his faux achievement. "It was nothing. Well, that's not true, it was something. Otherwise, I would have been on-time."

"That's incredible," said Andy in awe. "But aren't you allergic to cats?"

"Yes... that's why it took so long." Everything that spewed from Nick's mouth was utter bullshit, but he was sure that Andy would fall for the ruse.

"That makes perfect sense. I'm so sorry for bringing up the fact that you were late."

"You're forgiven," replied Nick, gesturing with his hand as if to bless Andy with forgiveness.

The two stared at each other, as if waiting for the other to say something. This stare down proved both awkward and a waste of time as both believed that the other was on the brink of saying something else. After a few more silent seconds, Nick finally spoke.

"Andy, is there something you need?"

"Oh, yes... all the servers are down, and everyone is panicking," replied Andy, finally breaking his gaze.

"Why would you wait this long to tell me!"

"Well, I was on my way to find you, then I did. Then you got mad at me for calling you a bitch, which I swear was supposed to be a joke. Then you told me how you rescued a cat, and now I am here explaining why it took me so long to tell you," replied Andy rapidly.

Nick looked blankly at Andy, both of his hands gripping the sides of his waist, as if to reprimand a troubled child. Nick stared in silence, unsure of what to even make of Andy's reply.

"Well... that's fair. Um... maybe we should get work?"

"Yeah, alright. Let's go," said Andy, as the two walked casually to their respective desks.

For roughly the next five hours, the two men worked diligently to get the servers running once more. In truth, the problem was not a major one. The extreme amount of time was simply because Nick lacked any experience with server malfunctions. He had never had a problem before, and so when faced with one, regardless of the severity, he was ill-equipped.

By 2pm, the servers were up and running again; and both men were in much need of a break. Nick felt his stomach churn as he longed for some sort of sustenance. Due to his late start, he had forgotten to pack his usual roast beef sandwich. For ten years that had been his sandwich of choice, and for the first time he was without it.

"Hey, did you want half of my sandwich," said Andy, as if reading Nick's mind.

Nick looked over, still holding his stomach. "What kind is it?"

"Egg salad."

"You disgust me," said Nick, turning his face away. "I'll just go out for lunch."

"Good choice. This sandwich is disgusting," said Andy, spitting a mouthful out in the garbage.

"Andy, I know you love the sandwich."

"I do. I don't know why I just did that." Andy stared desperately at the chewed up piece of food in the garbage.

"It's because you're weak."

Without another word, Nick stood up and headed for the exit. As Nick continued past the lobby, he quietly searched to see if Sam was around. Perhaps if she was, he would invite her to lunch with him.

Nick knew that he would never actually ask her, but the thought that he could was a sobering one. To his dismay, she was not at her desk. He thought about waiting a bit, or perhaps even asking around, but the idea of doing so seemed very stalker-like and immediately turned him off. So, Nick decided to press forth alone in search for a roast beef sandwich.

Nick's stomach pained him. He was used to following a certain routine, anything else simply did not agree with him. Nick trudged across the street, hoping that the sandwich shop was nearby. Little did he know, that the events that were soon to unfold would change his life forever.

You see, everything that had happened on this day was leading to this specific moment. Had the servers never gone down, he would never have taken his lunch so late. Had he woken up on time, he would have been early for work and packed his usual lunch, thereby eliminating his need to search for a sandwich. And had he not been late, he would have worn his usual shoes and not the uncomfortable, floppy sneakers that he was currently wearing. These 'mishaps', if you will, were setting him on course for a life-altering event.

As Nick trudged down the sidewalk, he noticed the sandwich shop on the other side of the road. Nick quickly dashed toward his goal, sprinting with pace that could rival even an Olympic athlete. As he reached the edge of the road, his shoes got the best of him. Nick tumbled over, knocking the woman in front of him onto the sidewalk. Nick lay sprawled out in the middle of the road. His body ached, but his pride hurt far more. As Nick got up slowly, hoping to apologize to the woman he had knocked over, he was unknowingly welcomed by impeding traffic.

And then everything went black.

4

THE STORY OF RON

He was very much different from his friend, Nick. The most noticeable difference was that he was quite tall. Well, he was tall in comparison to Nick, who was, at best, slightly below average in height. The other main physical difference was the colour of their skin. One was dark and the other was much lighter. However, if you had asked Nick or Ron what made them so different, neither of them would have noted either of these things.

Ron would have said that the main difference between the two was that he was more outgoing and sociable, whereas Nick preferred the company of just a few. If you had pressed Ron further on the subject, he might have even said that Nick had the tendency to be uptight, but that it was simply Nick's way of hiding his feelings.

If you were to ask Nick about what he thought about Ron's comparison, Nick would most likely grumble, or shrug – though he would not disagree. However, Nick would add something to the list. For Nick always believed the biggest difference between himself and Ron was not their height, skin colour, or their sociability and lifestyle habits. Their biggest difference was in fact hope. You see, Nick both admired and envied his friend for his ability to be hopeful, not in himself, but in others. It was actually hope that brought Nick and Ron together.

Ron had moved into Nick's neighbourhood at the age of seven. Without any friends or siblings to keep him company, Ron had hoped that he might find a friend. Then he met Nick. At the time, Nick was sitting glumly on the sidewalk as his sister Kate kicked a football against the side of the house.

"Nick, come play with me," said Kate.

Nick looked toward his sister, who had stopped kicking the ball.

"I don't want to play. I'm tired." Nick resumed his lethargic state and rested his head against the palms of his hand, as if he was so tired that he could not hold up his own head.

And that's when he came over.

"Can I play?" These were the first words that both Kate and Nick heard from the boy who would eventually become one of the most important individuals in both their lives. "I'm Ron. I just moved here."

Nick stood up swiftly. His small arms crossed, his eyes glaring at the new boy who stood much taller than him. "You can, but we play by my rules."

"I thought you didn't want to play, Nick?" asked Kate, as she moved in closer.

"I didn't want to play your game. This is my game."

"I'll play anything," said Ron.

The sun began to break through the clouds, and both siblings looked toward the boy, surprised by his willingness to comply. Ron continued to stand in front of them   a smile plastered on his face. That was the thing Nick remembered the most: how Ron smiled when they began to play. It may have just been a smile, but it was the sincerity behind it that caught Nick off-guard. It was a hopeful smile. It was the kind of smile that seemed to imply "*I believe in you.*" And Nick had never believed in people. Nick knew sincere people existed, but it was Ron's readiness to trust the siblings that made Nick believe.

5

THE STORY OF
WHEN NICK WOKE UP

That is how Nick died. Lying motionless, unable to open his eyes, Nick was sure that his life was over. However, he soon realized that his ability to think about death proved he was still alive. That and the fact that a woman's voice shouting *Nick* kept droning in and out of his mind.

As Nick mustered up the strength to open his eyes, he found his sister standing over him. "Nick, you're awake," said Kate, with a sigh of relief.

"Yes, should I not be?" replied Nick, unsure why his sister was standing over him.

"Nick, do you remember anything?"

Nick sat up, perplexed by the question. He began to scan his environment rapidly, trying to take it all in. White sheets draped over his aching body. Ahead of him lay nothing but a white silver chair and white walls. The entire room gave Nick an empty, uneasy feeling. And then he heard it — the beeping of a heart monitor. Confused, Nick turned cautiously toward the sound, staring up at the machine. "Why am I at the hospital?"

"There was a car accident," said Kate, grabbing his hand. Her eyes began to water as the words sank in.

"But I don't drive..." said Nick.

"You weren't driving. You were walking. Well, actually, you dove, while walking — at least that's what I've been told," replied Kate, as if she was trying to remember a story.

"Oh, that all makes sense."

"Really?"

"No! I have no idea what you're even talking about. Last thing I remember is crossing the street to get a roast beef sandwich. Speaking of which, I could use one right now." Nick clenched his stomach, but it did not pain him, nor did he actually feel hungry.

"Nick, this is serious! You could have died!" said Kate, punching Nick in the shoulder.

"Ouch! Why would you hit a man who is already in the hospital?" said Nick while rubbing his shoulder.

"Because... I love you... and I can't lose you... and you make me mad all at the same time." Kate bit her lip in an attempt to hold back the tears.

Whatever had happened had left her both scared and worried. Nick hated seeing his sister like this. He cared for her, although he hated admitting it.

"Kate..." The words trembled out of his mouth. He had no idea what to say, but he would say every word that he knew just to make her feel better. However, he was unable to continue as Andy came bursting through the door.

"Nick! I am so glad you're okay. Everyone at work is freaking out." Andy bolted over to him and hugged him tightly.

"Andy, get off. Why are YOU here?" shouted Nick, pushing Andy away.

"I heard about the accident, and then I heard that you didn't even get to eat your roast beef sandwich, and so I figured that I could bring you some food to cheer you up," replied Andy, holding up a roast beef sandwich.

"That is... such a waste of time, Andy."

"You're right. I'm sorry. I'll just get rid of it. I am so sorry to bother you. I hope you feel better," said Andy, as he slowly retreated to the door.

"Wait," said Nick, revealing a sudden sincerity in his voice.

Andy turned around in a hurry, a smile gleaming across his face. Andy always knew that Nick had a soft spot, and here he was, finally showing his vulnerability to him. Andy walked up to the bed, his hands reaching out to Nick's.

"Andy..." said Nick, extending his hand.

"Yes, do you need something?" Andy replied, excitedly.

"Yeah... leave the sandwich when you go," said Nick, snatching the sandwich away from Andy.

"Sure..." Without another thought, Andy simply put his head down and headed out the door.

Nick did not waste any time devouring the sandwich. You see, Nick did not care that he was in a hospital, nor did he care that he was sore from head-to-toe. His only real concern was the fact that he never actually got to eat his roast beef sandwich, and hoped that doing so would somehow make the world right again.

"What is the matter with you?" said Kate, slapping him across the shoulder.

"Again with the hitting. Why can't you understand that I am already in pain? I don't need to be reminded," said Nick, displeased that his eating had once again been interrupted with pain.

"Was that the Andy you always talk about?"

"Yes, I am so sorry you had to meet him. I actively try to avoid introducing him to other people. He always seems to just barge in. Plus, have you seen his face? I don't quite like it. Something about it makes me want to punch it." Nick clenched his fist followed by a jab-like motion. Nick never quite liked the idea of visualization, however, he did on occasion make exceptions. Nick continued to visualize Andy's face as he repeated various jab motions in front of him.

"Nick, he was nothing but pleasant, and he obviously cares about you."

"That's ridiculous. Andy is a plague."

"The man showed up to the hospital as soon as you were admitted. If you ask me, he cares about you."

Nick thought about it for a moment. Andy had come to his aid and more importantly brought the roast beef sandwich he so greatly desired. Yet, despite all of this, he was bothered by Andy's arrival. This had nothing to do with Andy himself, but rather he was unsure who else would show up to support him.

"I'm sure others will come visit soon enough. Andy just likes to pester me," replied Nick.

"Tom hasn't come."

"He hasn't?"

He could not stand the fact that Kate brought up Tom. He knew how she hated him and would look for any opportunity to bash him. Yet, there was a part of him that felt hurt, betrayed even. The thought of his friend not coming to see him hurt him deeper than he could have ever imagined. He always knew that Tom was aloof and unreliable, but he thought that he might make an exception when Nick's life was possibly at stake. At that moment, Nick began to doubt his relationship with Tom, his choice of friends, and most importantly, his ability to be a friend. Perhaps a near-death experience was exactly what Nick needed. Unfortunately, this metamorphosis did not last long, as Nick took another bite of his sandwich and forgot all about his previous doubts.

"So, what happened anyway?" asked Nick.

"Pardon?" said Kate, confused on the change of subject.

"How did I end up here? Why am I in so much pain? Is there a nurse in this bloody hospital, or are you now my caretaker?"

"They couldn't pay me enough to be your caretaker." Kate gave a cheeky grin.

"Very well, I don't blame you," Nick said with a shrug. Although Nick knew his sister was joking, there was a part of him that was hurt by the comment. That being said, Nick was far too proud to ever let his displeasure show.

Niiiiick...

"Yes?" Nick responded.

"I didn't say anything," Kate responded, rather confused.

"Yes you did. I heard you. You said, *Niiiiiiiiick*." Nick did his best imitation of the voice he had heard.

"Nick, I didn't say anything. It's been silent. Maybe you hit your head harder than we previously thought."

The idea of hearing voices terrified Nick. The last thing he wanted was for others to think he was ill, or worse, crazy. So, like any normal human being, Nick decided to lie.

"Got you," said Nick, pointing at his sister.

"Got me?"

"Yes, I was faking it. Just a little hospital humour."

It was clear by the look on Kate's face that she was not amused.

"Well, it's not for everyone."

"Clearly not," said Kate, her head shaking in disapproval.

"So, I was hit in the head?" said Nick, trying to once again change the subject.

"Right, I guess I should explain this all to you. Although it does worry me that you can't remember," said Kate.

Nick shook his head nonchalantly. While the voices and the fact that he could not remember anything did indeed scare him, Nick felt like it was his duty to avoid adding worry to his sister. Besides, by dismissing it himself, it no longer became real, but an afterthought in his life.

"Okay, so according to what I was told by the officers on the scene, you were walking across the street. There was a woman in front of you. A car came... it lost control... it would have hit the woman. You jumped and pushed her out of the way."

As Kate finished her story, Nick was unable to say a word. He sat there, replaying the words over and over, trying to make sense of it all. Could this really be true? Was this in fact what happened? As Nick sat wide-eyed, Kate finally spoke up.

"Nick?" said Kate, trying to break Nick's catatonic-like state.

"Yeah... I'm just trying to figure out what it all means."

"It means... Nick, you're a hero."

6

THE STORY OF HEROES

What factors define a hero?

The classics suggest that a hero is one who is able to overcome evil or adversity to achieve great feats. By these standards, the tales of Heracles, Perseus, and even Harry Potter are examples of classic heroism. In each of these cases, they took on tasks that could not be carried out by another. They overcame their trials and stood tall.

Nick, on the other hand, was lying flat on his back in a hospital bed. I know what you are thinking; how could Nick ever be deemed a hero? Perhaps our answer is not with Nick, but with the definition of a classical hero.

Modern tales define heroes as characters who despite the odds, triumph. Based on this definition, one could say that Nick did not perform a heroic deed. Do not get me wrong, I would love to give him credit. After all, the fellow needs a win. However, I cannot in good conscience condone deeming his act as an act of heroism.

While walking in Nick's uncomfortable shoes may constitute to some as a strenuous activity, the feat is not by any means heroic. Sure, the outcome of saving a life is heroic, but once you take into consideration the accidental nature of the situation, the heroics diminish, leaving nothing but an awkward and somewhat messy affair.

To Nick's benefit, he did not remember any of this. And so, in everyone's mind, he was a true modern hero.

An everyday Superman.

7

THE STORY OF QUESTIONS

"That doesn't really sound like me," said Nick, shocked that his very own sister was hailing him as a hero. "I mean, if you had said, 'Nick, you're an arse' or 'Nick, you're quite the frugal shopper,' I might have agreed with you."

Kate simply stared at her brother, unsure of what to make of his denial. Nick had never been one for heroics. His last heroic deed came at the age of nine. As the story goes, Kate was on a trampoline. She had been practicing somersaults and felt that she was in good form to do another, however, a stumble upon her initial bounce caused her to fall off the trampoline entirely. Luckily, Nick happened to be walking by, and his body acted as a cushion for his dear sister.

As the two siblings continued to stare at one another, Kate finally spoke up. "Yeah, that doesn't really sound like you."

"Thank you," retorted Nick. "There must be some sort of mistake. How could I have saved someone? I mean, could you really imagine me jumping in front of a car to save someone else's life? I barely want to help the people I know, let alone a complete stranger."

Both Nick and Kate began to laugh at the very thought of it all. Truth be told, it all seemed very absurd. The two siblings laughed harder than they had in years.

"I know what you mean. To think my brother could save anyone is absolutely ridiculous. I'm Nick... and I'm going to save your life today," mocked Kate, laughing as she imagined the scenario.

Nick's laughter quickly ceased. He was all for making jokes about himself, but as soon as anyone else joined in – especially if they enjoyed it – he was immediately turned off. Kate seemed unaware of his annoyance, as she continued to laugh, creating new scenarios in which her brother performed greater and greater heroic deeds.

"Okay, well you could give me some credit. After all, I just saved someone's life," said Nick.

His sister immediately quieted down. Her expression reverted back to one of deep concern as she mouthed the word *sorry*. Kate truly meant no harm against her brother. She loved him tremendously, and if he was indeed a hero, she could not be any prouder.

"I swear, you're just as bad as Andy," said Nick, in an attempt to retort against his sister's previous remarks.

"Eh, you hate Andy."

"You're right. That's an unfair comparison. No one is as bad as Andy."

As the words left his mouth, he began to reminisce about his bumbling co-worker. *What a fool*, he thought.

"Nick," Kate said.

"Yes."

"I am glad you're okay. I really am," said Kate, holding her brother's hand tight.

For a moment, Nick sat silently, a smile breaking across his face. It was rare for him to have such a genuine moment, but here he was having one with one of the most important people in his life. Looking into his sister's eyes, he knew how much she valued him.

After all, she had already lost her husband, and to lose her brother... well, that was something Nick did not want to think about.

"I am, too," said Nick, squeezing his sister's hand before finally letting it go.

Kate solemnly smiled before getting up from her seat. "I think we can probably check you out now."

"That seems awfully fast," said Nick.

"The doctor originally said your wounds were minor. The only concerning thing is you can't remember the accident, but I am sure if I tell the doctor that I am taking you, he'll be fine with it. So, I'll be right back."

The room was quiet, the only sound was the monitor beside him beeping which Nick thought was a good thing, seeing as it meant that he was still alive. It was all so very strange though. I mean, why was no one else here? Since he had been awake, not a single nurse or doctor had checked in on him; and on top of that, if he had really saved someone's life, he was sure there would be a bigger commotion rather than just Andy and his sister visiting him.

Nick continued to ponder the legitimacy of the whole story, until he heard his name again.

Niiiick

It seemed to both echo within the room and his mind. Could he really be hearing voices? This bothered Nick tremendously. Not because of the possible health concerns, but simply because admitting it would mean that he would have to spend even more time in the hospital.

Nick scrambled out of the hospital bed, quickly searching for his things so that he could leave. He was sure that if the hospital ran tests they would find something wrong with him. It was a chance he was not willing to take he needed to leave and leave soon. He scanned the room frantically, unsure of where they might have put his things. As he continued to search the room, he heard the door open.

"Well, I'm glad to see you're up and about, but you really should take it easy," said the man, glaring towards Nick who looked absolutely lost and ragged in his hospital gown. The man was short and lean, and wore a white coat — a clear indication that he must be the doctor.

"I was just stretching. Can never do enough stretching," replied Nick. Nick began to raise his arms and lift his legs in an awkward motion. Stretching was not something Nick did, so to use it as an excuse was a very poor idea.

"Relax, you're anxious to leave. I get it. I'm Dr. Tennant," the man said, as he reached out his hand. Nick reluctantly stretched out his hand, although he found the formal greeting strange, considering he was just a regular patient. It was nonsensical to him as to why he needed to get to know his doctor — especially because he was about to leave.

"It's not that I don't like the place, it's just I feel as if I could do more good outside... this place," said Nick, trying to defend his desire to leave. Despite the fact that he had every right to want to go back home, Nick felt as if it was an insult to the doctor if he were to vocalized this yearning. He felt that his desire to leave might seem as if he thought he was too good to receive their help, which was not far from the truth.

"Of course, a hero like you needs to be out in the world. Now, some people call me a hero, but I get paid to do what I do. You sacrificed everything to save a complete stranger. You're the real hero," said the doctor, tilting his head, as if to play the scenario in his mind. "Really makes you think..."

Nick stared at him, shocked that he would downplay the heroics of being a doctor. Nick saved a life, but he could not remember it. Did that mean he was any less of a hero? Here was a man who saves lives on a regular basis, and he was hailing Nick. Perhaps he really was a hero, Nick thought.

"Well, you do what needs to be done. You know what I'm talking about," said Nick, pointing and winking at the doctor. It was something he immediately regretted as he felt the gesture was both arrogant and narcissistic. There was no way the doctor would respond well to it. However, to Nick's surprise, the doctor smiled and winked back.

"You've got to be kidding me," mumbled Nick.

"Sorry, did you say something?" asked the doctor.

"No, just excited to be up and about again."

"You'll be out of here soon enough. I just need to run a quick examination." The doctor pulled out his stethoscope and various other instruments that Nick was unfamiliar with.

Nick began to panic. What if the doctor realized that he was hearing voices? Would he lock him up, and keep him around the hospital, trapped in this bed until the voices vanished? Nick did not like this scenario. However, what Nick failed to remember was that he had a foolproof way of getting out — all he needed to do was lie.

The doctor began poking and prodding as he examined Nick physically. Nick hated being touched, even by a doctor. That being said, it was his way out, and so he sat patiently as the examination commenced. It really did not take long, but then the doctor began to ask questions. *"Do you feel any dizziness, exhaustion, weakness, etc.?"* The questions poured out of his mouth with no end in sight. Nick remained calm and politely answered *no* to all of them. Finally the doctor asked him the question he was dreading.

"Have you been hearing any voices or unusual sounds?"

Nick sat awkwardly, scared that his mouth might lose control and spill the secret. Nick clenched his teeth and swallowed as he prepared to speak up. "Nope," he said, as his tension eased.

"That's good. You seem absolutely healthy, I mean, considering you got hit by a car," said the doctor. Nick chuckled politely, but the truth was, none of it mattered. He wanted to be discharged already, and this was taking too long for his liking.

"Does this mean I get to leave?"

"Yes, I don't see why not. Your stuff is in the closet. I'll just sign this form and you're free to leave as soon as you get ready," replied the doctor.

"Thank you," said Nick, bowing toward the doctor as he exited the room. As soon as the door closed, Nick jumped up in a hurry. He quickly rushed over to the closet and gathered his belongings. There was a sense of comfort as he began putting on his own clothes. It seemed as with each item gathered, a little bit of himself became whole again.

Nick reached down into a basket and pulled out his watch. It was the watch Ron had given him when they were both teenagers. He had worn it every day, and the thought of having it off for even a moment panicked him tremendously.

He remembered the day Ron had given it to him. They were only sixteen. Ron and Nick had been playing football on the pitch all day. Kate was there too, although she preferred to watch and giggle as the two boys tried to outdo one another. Part way through their game, Ron stopped and went over to his bag. Nick had no idea what made him so eager to stop playing. However, just as quickly as he left, he returned holding what was soon to become Nick's watch.

"What's this for?" questioned Nick, as Ron handed over the silver watch. "It's not my birthday for another month."

"It's not a gift, it's an apology..." said Ron.

"An apology for what?"

"For asking out your sister?"

Nick quickly turned toward his sister who looked petrified that Nick was not privy to her affair with his best friend.

"Are you mad?" asked Ron.

"Her dating anyone scares the hell out of me, but if it has to be someone, why not my best mate?" Nick said, shrugging his shoulders in acceptance of the new love.

"Nick, think of this watch as a promise. It's my promise to you that I will do everything in my power to make her happy."

"If this watch is your promise, you should have bought a more expensive piece."

As he stood there holding the watch, remembering his time with his late friend, he noticed something. Actually, he noticed a lack of something – there was not a single scratch on his watch. Nick wondered how this could be so. After all, he had been hit by a car, yet it looked brand new. Despite the lack of wear-and-tear, the watch was not working either. Both hands remained still, as if time itself was frozen. Nevertheless, Nick placed the watch back on his wrist. Nick did not need the watch to work, he just needed it to be where it belonged.

Nick gathered the rest of his belongings and placed them in the correct pockets. Wallet in the front left, phone in the front right, keys in the back right. As Nick gave himself a pat-down to ensure that everything was where it was supposed to be, a sense of comfort and consistency came over him. Things were finally starting to go back to the way they were. Well, as normal as things could be after finding out that he was now a hero. He was sure that this hero ordeal would blow over after a few weeks.

Nick walked toward the door and was about to exit the room when he realized something. He had forgotten to put on his shoes. Silly him, he thought. It was clear the accident had taken a greater toll on him than he had originally thought. It was not like him to forget anything- especially something as simple as shoes.

Nick walked back over to the closet in search of his shoes. They were sandwiched in the corner. Nick was forced to bend down and pull them out of the dark abyss that was the hospital closet. These shoes were terrible, he thought. He could barely walk in them.

And then it all came back.

8

THE STORY OF DENIAL

The memory of the accident flooded his mind. It had all come back. He was no hero, just a clumsy oaf wearing shoes that were far too large for him. He knew it was all too good to be true. He did not want to be deemed a hero to begin with, but to realize that that was not even the case hurt him deeper than he would like to admit. Nick clenched his shoes, hoping that perhaps this was all just a dream; that he would wake up and realize that he was still in his bed.

The door opened and Nick turned around swiftly.

"Nick, are you alright? You're taking awfully long in there." Kate walked into the room and headed straight toward Nick, who was staring mindlessly at the wall in front of him.

"Kate, what if I had been changing? You can't just walk into a room like that."

"Oh, I'm sorry, should I have galloped into the room, or maybe I could have skipped, or danced," said Kate, twirling in a rhythmic motion.

"Bloody hell, I don't need your jokes right now. Could you just be serious for a moment," Nick dropped his shoes and looked up at Kate. He could tell by her look that she was not impressed with his attitude, but what came next surprised him.

"I'm sorry," said Kate. "I guess, I didn't think before I walked in."

Nick was at a loss for words. His sister always had a witty response for everything, and despite the fact that Nick was a year older, she never had a problem putting him in his place. Nick wondered why she was being so nice. Could it be because of his heroism?

"Why are you being so nice?" asked Nick. "Is it because I'm a hero?"

"You really do say some silly things sometimes."

"Okay, now I am confused..."

Kate shook her head and smiled. "It's because you're my brother... Were you not aware of that?" her head gazing upon the floor as if she could not look at Nick while saying these words.

There she was, the old Kate. Nick found it hard to accept her innate kindness without a little sarcasm sprinkled in the mix.

"I have a question," said Nick, his hands trembling as he spoke.

"Yeah, of course. Ask away."

Nick wanted to tell her the truth behind it all. That he was not a hero, but a sham. Someone who had somehow taken credit for an act that he did not even mean. He could not be deemed a hero. There was not an ounce of heroism in his blood nor bones.

"Go on, you can ask me anything."

"If I wasn't a hero, would that be okay?" asked Nick, unsure of how to phrase the question.

"Well you weren't one yesterday, and I was fine with it," Kate replied.

Despite the seriousness of the situation, Nick could not refrain from letting out a chuckle. Feeling proud, Kate followed with a chuckle of her own. It was as if earning Nick's laughter was a trophy one Kate was more than proud to claim.

Nick fidgeted with his watch, trying to muster up the courage to tell his sister the truth. Yet, despite his desire to be truthful, he could not utter the words. It was as if saying them aloud would erase the deed from existence.

"Is everything okay?" asked Kate.

Nick did not have a response. Things were not okay, because everything was a lie that he desperately wanted to believe. However, deep down, Nick understood that all things must end, especially if they are not true.

"I'm not a hero." Sweat dripped from Nick's brow. The words were not meant to come out so readily, but he could not contain himself. Nick let go of his watch, as he awaited Kate's inevitable realization.

"Nick, we've been through this. You did a great thing. It's okay to accept it."

"I really didn't, it's all a big misunderstanding. I..." rambled Nick rapidly.

"Nick, please, calm down. I don't want to hear it anymore. You did a wonderful thing. Please, just accept it. The thought of my brother being hurt kills me. The only thing that gives me some sort of solace is knowing why it happened. You did it to save someone else. Ron never had that chance." Kate's eyes watered as she spoke.

Nick did not even think about how this ordeal might have affected his sister. She had already lost her husband to a drunk driver. She had gone through more than any person should. The last thing Nick wanted was to add more grief into her already difficult life. Nick looked into his sister's eyes and knew that now more than ever, she needed this lie. To Nick, a lie is only decent if it helps someone you love.

And so, Nick decided to do just that; lie. After all, he was sure that no one else would care about the incident.

"I'm sorry, you're right. But, Kate, I promise nothing will happen to me."

"Better not," replied Kate, wiping away a tear that had managed to fall.

Despite the difficulty, Kate smiled once more. Seeing this, it was not hard for Nick to follow suit. It was strange, but Nick quickly came to terms with the lie   something that would normally haunt him immensely.

"Come on," gestured Kate. "I have to pick up the children, and I think its best you stay with us for a while until you get back on your feet."

Nick looked at his feet and back at his sister. "I am not sure if you noticed, but I am already on my feet, and doing quite well with it, if I might add." Just for extra measure, Nick shook his feet to show that they indeed worked. Kate did not look pleased.

"Bloody hell, Nick, I know you can walk. I am just saying you might be better off staying with me until you feel better," said Kate.

"I am perfectly fine. Trust me, I'm okay." Nick grabbed on to his sister's hands. He hoped that perhaps that he could appeal to her emotional side with his longing, desperate eyes, and his intense, yet comforting hand grab. Nick was not one to fall for such cheap tricks, but he knew that his sister was too good of a person to not feel something.

Nick could tell that it bothered her to give in to his demands, as she refused to even look him in the eye, preferring to stare at the ground scornfully. However, Nick was determined to get his way - something that Kate knew.

"Alright, but at least let me drive you home," said Kate, shaking her head.

"Okay, but let me clarify. When you say drive me home, you mean my home, not yours."

"Bollocks, alright," said Kate, as she walked out of the room.

Nick followed as he shook his head. It did not surprise him that Kate would try and pull one over on him, but nonetheless, it annoyed him that she tried. The siblings walked through the hospital, not saying a word to each other. It was not because they had nothing to say, it was just that to Nick, a hospital was not the best place to start a conversation.

The ride home consisted of small talk   something Nick hated but Kate insisted on doing. According to her, that is just what people do. Apparently, small talk is a necessary ingredient in all relationships. Nick felt it was a nuisance, but humoured his sister anyway. Kate was very much aware of her brother's disdain for small talk, and so she quickly transitioned to stories of her children. Nick was even more bored. Nick loved his niece and nephew very much, but hearing stories of their 'achievements' bored him tremendously. After all, an *A* on a grade 5 science test did not seem like much of a feat. Nick felt quite confident that he could easily do the same. That was the thing about Nick. If he could do it, it did not impress him.

"And so at the end of it, she got a ribbon, which was nice," said Kate, after a lengthy story about Allison's track and field day. Nick was not paying very close attention to it, as his mind drifted to more important things such as the recent accident, his lie, and whether or not he left the sink running before he left.

Then something caught Nick's attention. "Wait, I'm confused by it all," said Nick, as he barely caught the end of the story.

"What is there is to be confused about? She participated in track and field and received a ribbon," said Kate, annoyed that her brother was not understanding the significance of her story.

"That's what I'm confused about."

"That she participated in track and field?"

Nick shook his head, as if to rearrange the ideas, hoping to get some sort of understanding. "You told me she came last," said Nick.

"She did."

"So then why did they give her a ribbon?"

"It was a participant ribbon!" said Kate, her annoyance now at an all-time high.

"What the hell is a participant ribbon?"

"They give everyone a ribbon, regardless of how well they do."

Nick could not fathom the words that were coming out of his sister's mouth. To Nick, all achievements should be earned, and nothing should be given. After all, nothing in life is just given to you. You have to work, fail, and try again. Nick believed in this philosophy quite adamantly. Which was slightly ironic given the fact that he recently lied about being a hero, or rather refused to correct those that had deemed him as such.

"So, let me get this straight. You're telling me they actually give ribbons to everyone, even if they come in last."

"Yes." Kate sat up dignified, as if she had spoken some universal truth on equity.

"That is the stupidest thing I have ever heard."

"You're stupid."

"Real mature there, Kate. But honestly, you're telling me that anyone can do anything and be rewarded for it?"

"Yes, they do it to encourage the children."

"They're breeding entitled pricks who will assume that anytime they do anything, they deserve some sort of reward or recognition. Then, when they get into the real world and they don't get the recognition they expect, they will throw a fit and act like an even bigger prick."

"Or you can look at it as you made a child happy, for even just a small moment," said Kate, hoping to convince her brother on the humanistic qualities of the act.

"I like my rationale better," said Nick.

"Of course you..." Kate stopped as the car rolled slowly toward Nick's home.

"Sorry, did you say something?" said Nick, awaking from yet another daydream. As Nick looked out the window, he saw what seemed like a swarm of people holding cameras and microphones outside his little home. People covered his driveway, yard and porch, while news vans blocked the road.

"What are they all doing here?" said Kate.

"Oh, God, I left the sink running. The house is probably flooded. I normally check but I was in a rush when I left." Nick began to panic and sweat as his heartbeat increased rapidly. The last thing he wanted was water damage to the house, anything else, he was sure he could deal with.

"It can't be that, I mean the house looks fine," said Kate.

"There could be internal water damage."

"Yes, all these people and cameras are here because of internal water damage in your ruddy little duplex," said Kate, shaking her head at the ridiculousness of her brother.

"You don't think it has to do with me being a hero and all, do

47

you?" Nick surprised himself with how easily the word *hero* rolled off his tongue. He had not fully accepted the idea, but he did like the way it sounded.

"Well look at that. It didn't take you long to start throwing the hero title around."

"I didn't…" muttered Nick, desperately trying to explain his use of the word.

"Relax, I'm kidding." Kate stuck out her tongue followed by a cheeky grin. Nick could not help but feel a little more relaxed knowing that his sister did not assume him to be the cocky self-assured asshole that he felt when dignifying himself as a hero. However, his relaxation quickly turned to panic when he realized that there were still people all over his lawn waiting to interview him.

"Nick, we have to make a decision. Do you want to come back to my place, or do you want to go in and deal with the reporters," asked Kate.

"They're all over my lawn. Do you know how hard I worked to make sure that my grass was neat and tidy?"

"Here, I'm just going to take you back to my place," said Kate, as she began to turn the car around.

"No, it's okay. What if we just hide and wait for them to leave?" Nick lowered his body as if to hide inside the car. He knew it was a terrible plan, but it was all he could think of under pressure.

"Nick, I'm just going to take you back to my place. I can take you home once everything clears up." Kate began to turn the wheel, but was no sooner stopped by Nick who stuck out his hand firmly, gesturing her to halt.

"It's okay, let's just wait."

Nick grabbed onto the wheel, and tried turning it in the opposite direction. However, this only made Kate grab on tighter, determined to win this tug-of-war. In their attempt to win supremacy, Nick's hand slipped off and ever so lightly pressed the horn. The horn droned for only a second, but it was enough to catch the attention of the horde of people waiting outside the house. Heads turned and all eyes gazed upon the car, like a shark to the scent of blood. Nick stared back, too terrified to turn away. In that moment, all eyes were on him, and he felt as though he was looking right back into all of theirs. Then, in one sudden motion, every reporter and cameraperson rushed toward the car. Nick desperately tried to hide, but he was also strangely curious to see what stations were covering his story. If he had to talk to reporters, he hoped that at the very least they were reputable stations. Nick scanned the area. He saw channel two, channel four, and of course, representatives from the local paper. Despite the fact that a horde of reporters was rushing to his car, Nick was very concerned that no larger newspapers or stations were covering his story. This not only disappointed Nick, but left him with a feeling of little self-worth. The feeling shortly passed, as Nick glanced at a reporter who he knew worked for the BBC. His feeling of disappointment was quickly replaced with that of terror, as the mob continued upon him.

"Look what you've done," said Nick, as he gripped the handle on the door tightly.

"What I've done? You were the one who pressed the horn. I tried to save you!" shouted Kate.

"Is this how it ends?" Nick looked into his sister's eyes as panic overtook him.

"Okay, you know that they're just reporters. We aren't going to die or anything," said Kate, in an attempt to place things back into perspective.

"You don't know what they're capable of."

"You're right. The really small woman with the microphone looks exceptionally sinister. She might just murder you here in cold blood." Kate chuckled as she shook her head. However, even she could not deny that the amount of reporters coming their way was a little intimidating.

Nick held on to his seat even tighter. The noise from the outside was roaring with a barrage of questions as camera flashes flickered in a constant wave. Nick knew that no harm would come to him, regardless if he was outside or not, but either way he was sure that he wanted to avoid the reporters at all cost.

"I know they won't harm me physically, but that doesn't mean they can't annoy me to death."

"What if we open the window and answer a few questions. Maybe they will go away," said Kate

"No, whatever you do, don't..." said Nick, in an attempt to talk his sister out of what he presumed was madness, or maybe a short-term cabin fever. However, his attempts at stopping her were futile, as both front windows began to lower. In an instant, hands from every direction reached through. It was like facing a horde of zombies ready to devour their prey. Except instead of zombies they were reporters, armed with their weapon of choice: microphones. This was clearly a far worse scenario.

"Is it true, you rushed over to save the woman after she tripped and fell?" inquired one reporter.

"What, no! It was an accident," said Nick.

"Reports suggest that you and the woman are now dating," another reporter added.

"I don't even know her. Until this morning, I didn't even know I had saved anyone," said Nick.

"Our sources tell us she is pregnant with your child. Can you confirm this?"

"I literally just said I didn't know her. Do you people listen to anything?" said Nick, annoyed with how inaccurate his heroics, regardless of being false, were being portrayed.

"You've been compared by many as a modern-day Superman. How does that feel?" said a small geeky woman wearing a Doctor Who shirt.

"Well, I actually don't mind that..." Nick envisioned himself performing similar heroics to the caped crusader. "But no, it was an accident. Please, just leave." Nick was beginning to feel guilty for taking even more credit.

The noise rumbled even louder. It was as if the horde would never cease. Nick was becoming increasingly exhausted after each question, as Kate simply sat there in a panic witnessing it all.

"No, I cannot fly, nor do I have any sort of magical powers. I am just a regular man. Seriously, where do you people come up with these things?" said Nick, as he attempted to push a microphone away from his face. "Please, help me." Nick turned toward Kate, desperation in his eyes.

Kate sat still—wide-eyed and in a panic. "Hold on and put on your seat belt," said Kate, as she finally turned toward her brother who was fending off reporters with a book he had found on the floor. Kate revved up the engine and in an instant, the crowd backed away from the car.

"Why didn't you do that all along?" asked Nick, both pleased to have gotten rid of the swarm, and annoyed that it had not happened earlier.

"I only just thought of it now. Doesn't matter, let's go." Kate put the car in drive and pulled away from the crowd.

Nick looked back for a moment. The crowd of reporters began to fade and blur with the distance. He was relieved to be rid of them, but feared that they might be back.

"Kate."

"Yes."

"Thanks for getting me out of there."

"Not a problem," responded Kate with a grin.

"Kate."

"Yes, Nick."

"Next time you come up with a plan to get us out of a jam, just ignore it and sit there instead," said Nick, in a more haughty tone.

"You're welcome, again," replied Kate, as she shook her head and continued to drive.

9

THE STORY OF
SECRET IDENTITIES

The burger joint was surprisingly empty, as Nick and Kate sat at a two-person table in the corner. The whole place reeked of grease and body odour, and with its dim lighting, one would not be wrong to assume that the place belonged in a dodgy horror film. Nick took a bite of his hamburger. He's always had a love-hate relationship with fast-food. He loved eating it, he hated the feeling of disgust he felt after. The horrible thing was, Nick was never satisfied with the amount either. If he ate a little bit of fast-food, he still felt hungry. If he ate a lot of fast-food, he felt sick. There was no happy medium.

"I will never understand how you don't like chips," said Kate, as she grabbed the bag of chips that came with his meal.

"They're just fried potatoes. I don't see the appeal," said Nick, as he ate the last bite of his burger.

"You don't see a lot of things, my dear brother."

Nick smiled hesitantly, but in truth, he was not listening. He had once again failed to find the happy medium in fast-food eating. "It's never enough." Nick crumpled up the wrapping and placed it in front of him.

"What is?"

"The food?" replied Nick, as if to let his sister in on his fast-food dilemma.

"We can get you another burger if you like."

"I'll just end up feeling sick, followed by much self-loathing," said Nick. "By the way, where are your kids?"

"They're with the neighbour," said Kate. "Did you really think I'd just leave them by themselves?"

"Well you might as well have. You left them with a neighbour," said Nick smugly.

"Steve is very helpful, and a wonderful person. He has a son who is Anthony's age, and he often comes over and helps me out when I need things. I do the same for him."

Nick was speechless. He had never heard of a neighbour, let alone a *"Steve"*. He knew she had neighbours. He wasn't so idiotic as to assume that the homes on either side were empty. Nick was simply unaware that his sister socialized with anyone else.

"Who is Steve?" asked Nick, still unable to fully comprehend the notion that there was a Steve.

"I just told you, he's the neighbour," said Kate, rather confused.

"No, what I am saying is, is there a Steve and Mary, Steve and Heather, or even a Steve and Craig?"

"If you are asking if he is married, the answer is no. He and his wife, or I should say ex-wife, divorced a few years back."

"And you're okay with leaving your children there?"

"I've known Steve for a few years now, and he is a very kind and sweet man," said Kate defensively.

The burger joint may have already been near-empty, but to Nick, it seemed as if the room had somehow gotten even more quiet. Nick only knew this to be untrue as he could still smell the body odour of the large gentleman   if you could call him that   who sat just a few feet away. Nick stared at the man, for just a moment. His large belly stretched his shirt beyond its normal size, enough that his gut was visible. Nick was very much mortified by the scene. Nick did not care too much about personal appearance, but he did believe that it was important for people to look presentable — something this man was clearly not.

"I just can't believe you left your children with a man."

"What difference does that make?"

"What if he's a pedo?"

"Nick!"

"I'm just saying, he could be. You never know these days," said Nick.

"He's not a pedo! And if it bothers you so much, just come over and meet him, you can see for yourself."

Nick hesitated for a moment. He did not really want to go to his sister's house. Not that he did not love his sister or his niece and nephew, he just preferred the quiet, and her house was anything but quiet.

"It's okay. I believe you," lied Nick, in order to get himself out of the engagement. Nick was not one to lie, but he had already lied about the hero thing, so he figured that he might as well keep going. "What kind of name is Steve? I mean, clearly his parents are a little off to name him Steve."

"It's actually quite a common name. You could say it is just as common as Nick." Kate smiled smugly at her ability to turn the tables on her brother.

"I disagree. Plus, you know what kind of people are named Steve? People like him," said Nick, as he pointed to the large man with the smelly body odour.

"Excuse me," called Kate, gesturing toward the large man. The man turned around – albeit very sluggishly.

"Yeah."

"By chance, is your name Steve?" asked Kate.

"No." said the large, smelly man, as he took a sip of his extra-large drink.

"What is your name?" asked Kate once more.

"Nick," bellowed the man.

Kate turned toward Nick, a haughty smile stretched across her face. Nick pretended to ignore her, but he could not help but feel irritated that his comments had backfired. Luckily, for Nick, Kate was not one to rub it in, and so, she changed the subject.

"Nick, where are you going to go, because you certainly cannot go home?"

Kate had made an excellent point something he hated to admit. Nick had nowhere to go. His home was being watched by the plague that is the media, and his only other choice was the chaos that is his sister's home.

"What if I took you to that Andy fella's home? He seems like a good bloke."

"Do you hate me? Because you must if you would suggest such a preposterous thing. Honestly, if I didn't know any better, I would have thought that you were the one hit by a car," said Nick.

"What's so wrong with Andy? All you ever say is that he is annoying. That's not enough of a reason to despise someone."

It became very clear to Nick that his sister was right. His complete disdain of Andy stemmed from nothing but a few small annoying habits. Overall, Andy was a good man helpful, considerate, and hardworking. There was absolutely no reason for Nick to feel the things he felt. However, by now you must have realized that Nick is a stubborn ass, and his views could not be swayed by a silly thing like logic.

"Well, I think he is. Perhaps you haven't properly witnessed the grand scope of his annoyance. I assure you, Kate, his idiocy will baffle you," said Nick, his frustration cooling down.

"Maybe so, but I am sure he would be there for you in an instant."

Nick was particularly taken aback by those last words. His sister truly believed that Andy would be there for him. His sister never believed any of his friends or acquaintances, save Ron, were good friends. She often cited their unreliability and selfishness as roadblocks to friendship. Nick wanted to prove her wrong.

"I'll go to Tom's. I'm sure he'll have me," said Nick, as he took a sip of his drink. Nick kept his head down, as he was far too afraid to look his sister in the eye after muttering Tom's name.

"Absolutely not! Tom is the worst!" shouted Kate.

"All I heard was absolutely. Thank you. You can drop me off."

"Honestly, Nick, I am not leaving you with that mental case of a friend," said Kate, becoming increasingly frustrated by her brother's poor decision-making.

"Why not? It will be the last place any reporter would think to go," said Nick, as if to provide some sort of logic to his clearly emotionally-based decision.

"That's because the reporters probably already know the waste of life that is Tom," Kate shot back. Her temper was rising, however, it did not come from a place of anger, but rather a place of concern.

"Well that seems a little excessive," said Nick.

"I'm sorry. But there has got to be an alternative that works for you. Okay, I'll tell you what, call Tom and see if it's okay. If he answers and he says its fine, I'll drop you off immediately."

Nick was faced with a double-edged sword. On one hand, if he refused to call, his sister would then refuse to drive him to Tom's. Thus, he would be forced to stay at his sisters, or worse, Andy's. However, if he did call Tom and he didn't answer – and he wouldn't, because Tom is a selfish ass who only calls when he needs something – he would once again be forced to accept his sister's offer. Kate had clearly thought this proposition through, as Nick noticed her lips curl into a grin. For just a moment, Nick thought that he had lost this battle of wits; but, it should be noted that Nick himself was capable of trickery and wit.

Nick picked up his phone and dialed Tom's number. The phone rang, but of course, there was no answer. After a few more rings, Tom's voicemail came on, his voice echoing through the phone. "Hi, it's Tom. I'm probably not too busy to answer my phone, and I will not get back to you." The phone beeped awaiting a message, but Nick simply froze. What was he to do? Tom had once again failed to deliver and now his sister would use this as ammunition for her hatred toward Tom. Nick, however, would not go down so easily.

"Hey Tom, it's Nick. What are you up to? ... Oh, okay. So you wouldn't mind me crashing at your place? ... Oh, that would be great. See you later, Tom... ha-ha – you too. Take care now, Tom." Nick's voice trailed off. He desperately hoped that his sister bought into the lie, but he knew his acting was not anything special. Nick never quite grasped the concept of acting, as he was far too much of a realist to understand the point of pretending.

"Okay, I guess you win. We'll go to Tom's," said Kate, as she changed route toward the home of Nick's aloof friend.

Nick was stunned. She had bought into his lie. Was it that easy to lie? Perhaps this hero thing could be easy after all, Nick thought. If he could trick his sister into taking him to Tom's, he could surely convince the world—or at least the city—that he was a hero. As Nick imagined the power of the lie and the rewards he could reap, his conflicted ethics got the best of him. Nick had never realized how much he wanted to be a hero until the chance to become one was thrust upon him. Alas, Nick knew that he couldn't willingly accept the title nor the rewards, as it was not justly earned. After all, what is a hero if not just?

The car pulled in front of Tom's place—a rustic bungalow that belonged to Tom's father. Tom's father had passed away and left him the place many years ago, and Tom had lived in it ever since. It was an old, rundown place. Nick was sure that at one point in time it looked nice, but it was clear that with the passing of time and Tom's lethargic attitude, the once quaint home was nothing more than four very damaged walls.

"I cannot believe you would rather stay here than with me. Honestly, if you weren't my brother, I'd be terribly insulted," said Kate.

"Well, don't let a silly thing like blood get in the way of you being insulted," shot back Nick.

"Oh, shut it, Nick. I mean, I understand the appeal, in a weird way," said Kate, glaring at the home, as if prolonged staring might change the visual appeal.

"You do?" Nick was quite sure that his sister did not understand the appeal of Tom's house. For her to understand the appeal, she would first have to understand that staying with her is like a circus, but instead of freaks, they were children—which was practically the same thing to him. For his sake, and his sister's, he desperately hoped that her sudden understanding was simply a misguided thought provoked by her desire to bond with her brother.

"Well, yes it's rundown and dirty, but it's a bachelor pad – in a loose sense of the term. No obligations, just freedom. In a weird way I'm a little jealous."

Nick could not help but feel sorry for his sister. He never thought about the fact that she was forever stuck in the circus, all by herself. Sure, Nick came by and helped out from time-to-time, but his sister lost her freedom the day she lost her husband. "I guess you've got a point," said Nick, unable to think of anything else to say. "I guess I'll head inside now. Thanks for everything, Kate. It means a lot, really."

"Not a problem. I just hope you feel better and know that I am here if you need anything," said Kate, as she waved him off.

Nick smiled at his sister before opening the car door to venture into the home of his friend. Nick was particularly excited about having some personal space, especially after the crazy day he had just endured. However, there was a part of him that felt sad to leave his sister. He knew that she really just cared; too much sometimes, but cared nonetheless.

"Nick," Kate called through the car door window. Nick turned around, unsure if he had perhaps forgotten something in the car. "Next time you pretend to have a fake phone call, make sure the person observing can't hear the message beforehand. And oh, work on your acting, dear." Kate grinned from ear-to-ear, as she watched her brother's awestruck face.

Nick stood absolutely still as he watched his sister drive off. She had known the whole time that he was lying, and yet here he was, exactly where he wanted to be. For a moment Nick wondered whether Kate admired his persistence or perhaps she knew his stubborn nature all too well. Either way, she had given in to his demands, albeit reluctantly so.

Nick walked up to the door and knocked, unsure of how Tom might take his boarding request. Nick waited, waited, and then waited some more. Perhaps his knock was too light, Nick thought. So, Nick reluctantly rang the doorbell. He hated ringing doorbells, as he found the sound to be a bit of an annoyance. Knocks were a far more appropriate tool. Nick waited, waited, and then waited some more. Once again, no one came to the door. Tom must not be home, Nick thought, realizing that his sister's offer might have been the better of the two deals. Nick refused to lose hope though, not because hope was a virtue he possessed, but mainly because he did not want to admit that going to Tom's was a mistake. Tom was lazy, forgetful and just all-around careless. Knowing this, Nick assumed that the door must not be locked. After all, to take the time to lock something means that one must first have the desire to care and protect something, and Tom didn't care for anything.

Nick pushed the door and with little effort, the door swung open. Nick quietly crept in as to not startle his friend. The house reeked of stale pizza and various types of cologne. Nick could not distinguish the exact fragrance, but knowing Tom, the title was pseudo-sexual, and probably cost quite a bit. Nick did not care about cologne. After all, if Nick wanted to smell good, he had soap — ironically, the same soap that Tom sells. The house itself consisted of painted grey walls. Nick supposed that at one time they must have been white, but the lack of upkeep had turned them grey over time. Nick continued to walk through the house quietly, as to not make a sound. "Ah, you wankers!" Nick heard from the living room. Well, that clearly answers my question on whether or not Tom was home, Nick thought, as he walked toward the noise.

"Tom!" bellowed Nick, as to make Tom aware of his presence.

"Oh, for fuck sakes," yelled Tom, as the sound of something crashing on the floor shortly followed. Nick was not too fond of his friend's incessant vulgarities. He found it both tasteless and a bit embarrassing. After all, to Nick, cursing required a loss of emotional control, something that nearly never happened to him.

Nick rushed into the living room to confront his friend. "Tom, it's me, Nick, just in case you forgot my voice. Not that you should forget my voice. I mean, we see each other at least once a week. Then again, you never have been good at paying attention to detail," babbled Nick, as he moved closer to his friend who seemed to be fixated upon a video game.

"Nick, what brings you about?" said Tom, his eyes still glued to the television screen.

"Did you not get any of my messages? And why didn't you answer the door?" Nick stood, his arms pressed against either side, like an angry parent scolding their child.

"I'm playing a game, bugger-off. I don't disturb you during one of your hobbies," Tom shot back.

Nick stared at the television screen. Tom was playing some sort of shooting game. Nick did not know too much about videogames, but he could tell the genre. After all, Tom firing his auto-rifle and spraying down what he described as 'newbs' was a clear indication that Tom was playing a shooter.

"I don't have any hobbies," said Nick.

"Exactly. So you wouldn't understand," said Tom sardonically.

Tom had made a valid point. Nick did not have any real hobbies. Then again, Nick did not classify videogames as a real hobby, but rather a distraction for the lazy. This is something that many people, including Tom have argued against vehemently. While Tom was indeed lazy and wrong about many things, when it came to arguing about videogames, he came across as reasonable, logical, and dare I say... intelligent.

"Well, what about my messages?" said Nick.

Tom picked up his phone with one hand, making sure to leave the other hand on the controller, as a driver might do at the helm. "Oh, well look at that. You got hit by a car," said Tom nonchalantly, scrolling through the messages.

"Thanks for your concern. Really, it means a lot."

Nick could not help but be offended by his friend's apathy. After all, had it been Tom who was hit by a car, Nick would have shown more concern. At the very least, he would have asked him how he was.

"It really isn't a big deal," said Tom.

"I was *hit* by a *car*. I was in a *coma* for roughly thirty minutes," said Nick, exaggerating the words hit, car and coma in order to draw emphasis on the seriousness of the situation.

"I was hit by a car. It's really not a big deal," said Tom. Despite the seriousness in his words, he seemed relaxed. The very thought of the incident gave Nick anxiety – yet, Tom was as cool as ever.

"You were?" Nick had never heard that Tom had been hit by a car. Upon first hearing it, he assumed that Tom was playing a trick; but after no response, Nick assumed his statement to be true. "When did this happen, Tom?"

"Which time?"

"It happened more than once?" said Nick, even more shocked that an incident such as being hit by cars numerous times had failed to ever be mentioned.

"It happened three times actually. First time I got the car, second time I got this tele, and the third time happened a few weeks ago. Got me this video game system. Pretty sweet isn't it."

"Wait, how? Why? I'm rather confused. Do you sue these people after you've been hit?" said Nick, flabbergasted by his friend's hidden affairs.

"No, after I've been hit, I just hold my head, or leg or something, and say that I'm hurt and tell them if they give me money and I won't report them." Tom glanced toward Nick and smirked as if he was letting Nick in on a secret.

"So you scam these people?"

"No, it's not a scam. I actually let the car hit me. You have to make it believable," said Tom.

Nick stared at his friend, slightly disturbed by the stories he had just been told. It was clear that Tom was a bad influence, and overall just a horrible human being. Yet, this idea had only just dawned on Nick. Tom was not a good friend, nor was he even a good member of society. It was as if Nick just saw everything in a new light. However, just as quickly as this new light came, it vanished with the shrug of Nick's shoulders. Nick would not let a few jarring stories change his relationship with Tom.

"Okay, forget about that right now. Actually, no, how are you? Don't answer that, I just had to ask," rambled Nick, remembering that he at least needed to ask Tom if he was okay to be deemed a good friend.

"I have no idea what you are going on about, but I'm hungry. Let's get food. You can pay with your accident money," said Tom.

"I don't have any accident money. I'm not suing anyone." Nick's nostrils flared, as he became increasingly annoyed with Tom's lack of concern.

"Well then you have made a huge mistake," said Tom, his attention once again on his television.

"Tom, I have some serious problems. I have been hearing voices." Nick could not believe that those words had even left his mouth. He had been afraid to admit that the voices he heard were real, and that perhaps it had just been a ringing in his ear   a side-effect from the accident.

"A lot of people hear voices in their head, Nick," said Tom.

"They do?"

"Yes, it's called your conscience, just ignore it."

"I'm serious, Tom. I've been hearing voices calling my name like, *NIIIIICKKK!*" Nick imitated the voice in his head as best as he could, but to any observer of this act, the natural conclusion would be that Nick was clearly insane. Tom, however, did not think that. Actually, Tom thought nothing of it, and readily ignored his friend's plea as a means to garner sympathy or attention.

Nick folded his arms, both out of frustration and because the house was very cold. Nick began to wonder if Tom had even paid the heating bill. Nick thought about bringing this up to Tom, but he knew that it would be of no interest to him. Tom simply continued to play his video game, as he cursed randomly into the microphone. "Of course you don't care," said Nick, throwing his hands up in frustration. "No one seems to understand this mess. I'm hurt, hearing voices, and being lauded as a hero. I don't get it."

Tom turned abruptly. A rare phenomena had occurred. Something that did not involve Tom directly peaked his interest. "A hero?" asked Tom

"Yes, apparently when I tripped and fell, I knocked over a woman, thus, saving her from being hit by a car. But what everyone fails to realize is that it was all an accident. I never meant to save her. Hell, I didn't even know she was in danger. I honestly just tripped. Of course, no one cares to hear the truth." Nick's breathing became heavy at the recollection of the events.

"Nick, you bloody fool," said Tom, a smile stretching across his face. Nick stared at his friend, wide-eyed, and curious as to what Tom would say next. "Do not deny anything. You're a hero and you need to embrace it. Forget what you think happened."

"You mean the truth?" Nick questioned.

"Forget the truth. What is truth, but one's perception and desire for meaning?"

"How philosophical of you, but in this case, I clearly fell and didn't mean to save anyone. Yet, everyone believes that what I did was so heroic and self-sacrificing instead of what it actually was: clumsy." Nick took a seat on an old television in the corner of the room. Tom did not have much furniture, save the armchair he was currently sitting in.

"Nick, my friend, do you not realize what you have quite literally stumbled upon? This event, whether intentional or not is a goldmine for our success," said Tom, his eyes widening as if to envision the future.

"Our success?"

"Well, I'll be your PR guy. After all, it is my field."

"When did you get into PR? What happened to the soap business?"

"The soap business is dead. No one needs soap anymore."

Nick was unsure of what Tom meant by this. Did he mean that there was an abundance of soap, and thus people did not need soap for a while? Or perhaps he meant that traditional soap was out of style, and there was a new kind of soap? Or did he mean that people were no longer using soap altogether? Either way, Tom's statement disturbed, confused, and worried Nick all at the same time. "I am not even going to pretend to understand what you mean by that. Anyway, back to the issue at hand, I don't want to be a hero, and I certainly do not need a PR guy."

"Of course you do! Think about what all this entails. Parties, money, fame, promotions." Tom waved his hands in the air with each word, as if to paint Nick a picture of all the things that could happen.

"I don't care about any of that. I like my simple life. I'm okay with it all." There was truth to Nick's words. He was more than okay with his life. He did not need much, and what little he did have he was content with. It was not like he was poor, sad, or without friends. To Nick, he had more than enough.

Tom was quite aware of Nick's simplistic nature. If he was going to sell him on this new life, he needed to say something that would make him think. Make him question all that he had and all that he had previously thought. After all, this was for Nick's own good, but more importantly to Tom, this was for Tom's own good. "Don't you want to be remembered? Don't you want to say that you have done something of some significance? This is your chance; and once you embrace it, other great things will follow. That woman you're obsessed with, Sandra, Sardine or whatever her name is... you can get her."

"Firstly, her name is Sam, and secondly, I am not obsessed with her," said Nick, both offended that Tom thought his love for Sam was obsessive; but flattered that Tom had paid enough attention to know that there was someone he liked.

"Either way, you can finally get her, and leave your mark on the world," said Tom.

To leave your mark on the world was a secret ambition of Nick's. There was a part of him that did feel unfulfilled. The part in all of us that questions our very purpose in life. The part of us that wonders that perhaps, there might be more to our lives than we had previously thought. While Nick felt that most things in his life were figured out, his purpose and desire to do something of importance was something that had always remained a mystery. However, here was Tom telling him that he could fill that void and solve the mystery that haunts us all. He could be a hero, and with it, he could be with Sam. He could truly have everything he ever desired. All he had to do was to accept what was already being thrust upon him.

"What would being a hero entail?" asked Nick.

"You just leave everything to me." A grin formed across Tom's face. It almost seemed sinister to Nick, had it not been for the fact that Nick could not imagine Tom being capable of anything sinister. ".Just know that from now on, you need to be different, you need to act different, because you are different. You are Nick. A hero of the people."

10

THE STORY OF FLYING

The tie clenched around Nick's neck. He hated having the thing so tight, but he hated the look of unprofessionalism even more. So, if a clenched neck was the side-effect of looking professional, it was a side-effect he would tolerate. As he put on his jacket, Tom's words echoed within his mind. "You are Nick. A hero of the people." Nick was not sure if he fully believed the statement. Nick knew the truth. His heroism was a sham. However, if people assumed he was a hero, who was he to deny them of their beliefs? After all, to deny one's beliefs was oppressive, and Nick did not want to be oppressive. At least that is how Tom rationalized the lie. Nick was but a willing puppet in Tom's master scheme.

Nick was okay with it all. If this surprises you, let me assure you, your surprise is nothing compared to how surprised Nick was of himself. Nick had always thought of himself as independent. However, since the accident, he found himself quite *de*pendent. Not necessarily on Tom, or any person for that matter, but on an idea. The idea that his life might be more than he had previously thought.

Today was Nick's first day back at work since the accident. He had no idea what to expect, but the very thought of the possibilities made him quite anxious.

Niiiiick...

The now familiar voice in his head called out, as Nick stepped out of the house. The voice did not bother him in the way it had done earlier. On the contrary, Nick had come to expect it. The voice, for whatever reason, called to him at specific times – usually in the morning, and then again at night. And so, just like Nick's life, the voice had become clockwork – a part of his usual routine.

"Yes, I am Nick. Thank you for once again reminding me," grumbled Nick, as he flung the strap of his bag around him. Nick placed his headphones in his ears and trudged toward his work. The sounds of The Gap Band's, *You Dropped a Bomb on Me* played, and Nick's mind wandered as his fantasies took hold. Birds chirped, the wind whistled, everything was exactly how Nick wanted. Well, mostly everything. You see, despite the wonderful fantasy that had begun, Nick saw people. Nick had never seen people before. Nick knew people were there, but he never noticed them during one of his daydreams. It was as if he transported all people to another dimension, or more likely, he transported himself in order to avoid them. People were never part of his plan, and yet, here they were. Everywhere he walked, he saw people, smiling, laughing, and being cheerful. For the first time in a very long time, he was beginning to notice humanity and all that made it great. It was all quite dreadful to Nick. He began to walk with greater pace, as he hurried his way toward his work.

Upon arrival, Nick was once again greeted with cheerful, smiling faces. However, this time they seemed to be mouthing something to him. Nick wondered whether this was all just a dream, or perhaps his fantasies were twisted by the accident. However, as Nick removed his headphones, neither the people, nor their smiles disappeared.

"Hey Nick, welcome back," said a tall, strange man in a grey blazer.

Nick had never met the man, so he had no idea why he thought it appropriate to speak to him. Nick supposed the greeting was meant to be pleasant, but he simply found the whole thing to be very awkward.

"Nick, so glad to see you up and walking. Glad to have you back," said a plump woman who Nick had only briefly met once in the copy room.

"Welcome back. So glad to have a real hero here," said another man, who Nick recognized instantly as the head of security.

And the compliments kept coming. It seemed that with every step he took, there was someone who had something nice to say. Nick was quite alarmed by the fact that every single person seemed to know him, yet he knew very few of them. What alarmed him even more was how much he enjoyed hearing the compliments. The once frightening smiles now invigorated him in a way that he never knew they could.

"Nick, I am so glad you are okay. When I heard what happened, I couldn't believe it," said a woman, as she threw her arms around him, burying her face in his shoulder. Nick's arms went limp. To be embraced in such a way, especially in public was foreign to him. That being said, Nick was strangely okay with it. There was something comforting about the whole thing. As the woman finally pulled away, Nick glanced down at the familiar face. It was Sam. The woman who had him mesmerized from the very moment he first laid eyes on her.

"Uh, you were worried... about me?" questioned Nick, still in awe that he had even touched a beauty such as Sam.

"Of course. I was watching the tele, and I saw that you had jumped in front of a car to save someone, and my heart sank immediately. I mean, she was a complete stranger, and you saved her. I always knew you were a selfless person." Sam let out a whimper, as if to show Nick just how scared and hurt she had been by the accident.

"I can't believe you even remembered me?"

"Of course, silly," said Sam, as she stroked his arm gently. "I mean, we have such great conversations. Like that one time... about that thing... the missing girl. That was such a great conversation. Really made me think, you know?"

Nick stood, stunned that Sam could even remember his name, let alone a conversation that had taken place between them. His heart rushed, and his face became flushed. If this was love, it had hit him hard and all at once. Despite his usual melancholy face, he could not help but smile.

"I am so glad you liked that conversation," said Nick, unsure of what he could possibly say in a moment like this. Little did he know that at this point, he could talk about children with cancer, or poverty in Africa and Sam would be entranced.

"Yes, I did. And you know, if you ever want to have another conversation, I am available to do so." Sam smiled so big it seemed to Nick that nothing could alter it, or rather, he hoped that nothing would.

"Yeah, absolutely. I mean, if they ever find the body of that missing child, I'll be sure to discuss it with you." As the words left his mouth, he immediately regretted it. Nick was not an expert in flirting by any means, but he was sure that mentioning dead children's bodies was at the very least frowned upon.

"Ah, yeah. For sure."

This surprised Nick, but he did not dare question it. In his mind, he had just gotten away with a dreadful comment, and to question it would only force him to relive the moment. And to him it did not matter, because Sam was laughing, and that was a rare treat. As a matter of fact, he had never seen her laugh, ever. He loved watching her laugh. He was sure that he could stay in the moment forever, just staring at her smile.

"Well, I look forward to it. The conversation. Not the dead child's body," said Nick, once again kicking himself for making a terrible comment. But once again, Sam simply laughed. And just like that, she was touching him again; her fingers making swirls along his forearm. If terrible comments led to affectionate touching, Nick was confident that he would only ever make inappropriate comments.

"Anyways, I best be off. I got a lot of catching up to do." Despite the obvious attention Sam was throwing his way, a part of him was afraid to act. As if he needed confirmation that Sam was indeed coming on to him before he could make any definitive move himself.

"Of course, wouldn't want to get in the way of a hero's duty," replied Sam.

"Ah-ha, yeah. Thanks. I'll catch you later." Nick strode toward the stairs. As the door to the stairs close behind him, Nick pressed his back against it and let out a sigh. That had been the most exhilarating, and tantalizing conversation he had ever had with Sam. As a matter of fact, he could not recall ever having such an overtly flirtatious conversation.

You see, Nick was used to very blunt, dry conversations. For example, his last real date occurred a little over a year ago, and the conversation went a little something like this:

Nick: How old are you?
Date: Thirty. You?
Nick: Thirty-five.
Date: Children?
Nick: No. You?
Date: Same. Want them?
Nick: Not at all.
Date: Same again.
Nick: Are you a fan of tea?
Date: Yes, quite so.
Nick: Great. Do you like steak?
Date: No, I'm a vegetarian.
Nick: Okay, this isn't going to work out.
Date: Agreed, but we tried.
Nick: Yes, take care now.

And that was the entire date. Interestingly enough, Nick later admitted to his sister that he may have been a bit rash in his decision not to pursue a second date. After all, it was not like Nick had many admirers. And that is what made his interaction with Sam so interesting. Despite his awkward blunders and his nervous dry humour, she seemed interested. No longer was he pursuing her, but rather he was being pursued – a concept that was quite foreign to him.

Nick climbed the stairs and reached the second floor. Once again, he was bombarded with various well-wishers and admirers. Some even gave him presents. As he reached his desk, Andy spun around to say a few words. "Hey Nick, glad to see that you're back," said Andy with a smile. And that was all he said. Nick was particularly confused by this. Here were strangers doting over him and his heroics, and yet Andy – the most overly affectionate human he had ever met – was not reacting in the same way.

"Andy, that's all?" said Nick, hoping to garner a little more enthusiasm in him. Nick was unsure as to why it bothered him so much. After all, he hated the fact that Andy doted over him so much. And yet, today when he expected the attention, he was not receiving it.

"I'm sorry, did you need something? It's your first day back, just take it easy. I'll handle most of the work," said Andy, once again very calmly.

Nick stared at his co-worker, confused by his sudden transformation. "No, I guess I don't, Andy. Thanks."

"Not a problem."

As Nick continued to stare at Andy, wondering why he was not acting like everyone else, he failed to notice the mountain of presents and gift baskets that were left on his desk. His work place had become a strange, unrecognizable fantasy. And it was this very thought that exhilarated him.

For the rest of his workday, Nick did not do any actual work. Most of his time was spent sorting cards and presents, and then indulging in the various chocolates and fruits within the baskets. Nick had become so caught up in everything that he had even missed lunch. Surprisingly, this did not bother him in the slightest. It was as if Nick was being sustained by the adoration.

Nick glanced at his watch to check the time. The blasted thing was still broken. Nick flicked it, hoping that perhaps a little flick was all it needed to start again. However, upon flicking, Nick's head began to throb.

Niiiiiiiicccccckkkk

The familiar voice droned in his mind. While Nick had become accustomed to the voice, it was strange to hear it in the afternoon. As Nick clenched his desk, as if to transfer the pain out of him, he heard another voice come from behind him.

"Nick, are you okay?" said Andy.

The pain finally began to subside, and Nick regained a sense of normalcy. "Yes, everything is fine. Just had a splitting headache."

"If you need anything for it, just let me know."

"Thanks, Andy. I'm fine."

"Well, it's five, so we can leave now if you like. If you need a ride home, or to your sister's or anywhere, I'm here," said Andy reassuringly.

Nick pondered for a moment the kind gesture. He hated accepting favours from anyone, but he could not deny that the offer was tempting. Truth be told, his hesitancy was linked to the simple fact that he did not feel close enough to Andy to accept his offer. That is, he did not consider him to be a friend.

"No, I'm fine. My buddy, Tom is coming to pick me up. Have you met Tom? Great bloke," explained Nick, as if the words were meant to convince him more than Andy.

"Okay, not a problem. Just thought I'd offer." Andy replied as he headed out of the office.

Nick waited for Andy to disappear from sight before he pulled out his phone and quickly dialed Tom's number. He was sure that Tom would not answer. It was not like Tom's unreliability was a secret. It was well known to everyone that Tom could not be counted on. Still, Nick felt it was his duty to call. He had told Andy that Tom was going to pick him up, and to not even try to get a ride home would feel like a lie.

As the phone rang, Nick paced, expecting the inevitable answering machine. To his surprise, he was warmly greeted by Tom. "Hey buddy, how are you? I have loads to tell you."

"Oh, well, I'm great. Thanks for asking. I was actually wondering if you would be willing to pick me up from work?" Nick's faced tensed as the words left his mouth.

"Of course. I'll be there in five minutes. I'll debrief you on everything once I'm there," said Tom.

The phone clicked off as Nick stood frozen, the phone still glued to his ear. Had Tom just agreed to pick him up? Nick removed the phone away from his ear, instead holding it in front of him at a distance – as if to see if the thing was even real. After all, it must all be fake for Tom to agree to a favour.

Nick slowly gathered his belongings and made his way down the stairs and to the lobby. The room was bare, not a single soul walking through. This was a strange occurrence, seeing as it was not late enough to warrant so little traffic within the building. But however strange it may have been, it still was nothing in comparison to the sense of joy that was slowly taking hold within Nick.

The accident, however horrible it may have been, propelled him to heights he did not even know existed. He had become a local celebrity – loved by his friends, adored by the masses. Tom wanted him around, Sam wanted to be with him, and his co-workers appreciated him.

As he stood in the centre of the lobby, he let out a sigh. Not of relief or exhaustion, but one of contentment. In that moment, Nick was more than just happy, he was undeniably fulfilled. His purpose, his very point of existence all meant something, and for the first time he believed it.

Nick felt his phone vibrate, and without even looking, he knew it was Tom telling him that he was here. Nick stepped out of the building and into his friend's beat-up vehicle.

"Well, you look like you had a good day," Nick did not look over, nor did he seem to acknowledge the comment. He simply put on his seatbelt and smiled. "I'll take that as a yes then," added Tom with a chuckle.

Tom revved the engine as they sped off toward Tom's place. Neither of them spoke, which was not unusual for the two given the fact that Nick hated talking in cars, but this time their silence was not out of awkwardness, but rather out of mutual understanding.

The car pulled into Tom's driveway. Still, neither of them spoke. After a while, Tom became increasingly agitated by Nick's inaudibility. "Are you going to just sit there silently, or are you going say something? I mean, the brooding hero thing can work, but I'd appreciate the heads-up," said Tom, turning his attention toward Nick, who was still staring silently out the window.

What happened next was both surprising and very out of character. Perhaps it was something Tom said, or maybe it was his current predicament, but Nick began to laugh. Not a quiet chuckle, nor a childish giggle, but a true, hearty laugh. And what made things even more interesting was the more Nick looked at Tom and thought about his heroism, the harder he laughed. Tom was at the moment, completely unaware of Nick's reason for laughing. However, despite the strangeness of the situation, Tom began to match Nick with an intense laugh of his own. Soon both friends were laughing hysterically, their voices booming through the car and into the neighbourhood.

"Why are you laughing?" asked Tom, his body exhausted from forcing a laughing fit.

Nick's laughter ceased as he regained control once more. "Don't you see?" said Nick, as if letting Tom into a secret. "I'm a fucking hero, Tom!"

To proclaim oneself as a hero without even the slightest bit of humility is in fact beyond arrogance. It is blind superiority. To some, that level of arrogance would be too much, but not for Tom. Tom revelled in his friend's newfound persona.

"Yes, thank you! You ARE a fucking hero, Nick! I am so glad you finally committed to this thing. But, why the sudden change of heart? Actually, don't tell me. I don't care. I'm just glad you finally figured out how lucrative this idea can be."

Nick smiled, his eyes crinkling at the thought of all the possibilities that could arise from this acceptance of greatness. "Do you really want to know what made me change my mind?"

"No, I just said I didn't. Didn't you hear me?" said Tom, quite confused by Nick's incessant need to explain reason and logic in every decision.

Nick blatantly ignored his friend's disinterest. His excitement had risen beyond a level he knew existed, and something as silly as Tom's apathy was not going to stand in the way of him and what he believed was his destiny.

"Tom, she talked to me," said Nick, the words bursting from his lips.

"Who? Are you hearing voices again?" asked Tom, not that he was concerned about the voices, but simply out of a need for clarification.

"No. Well, yes... but that is beside the point. I'm talking about *her*. Sam!"

"Haven't you talked to her before? I mean, I'm happy for you. I guess. But I don't see the big deal about a woman talking to you." Tom was unamused by the anecdote, and could not for the life of him see the point that Nick was trying to make.

".Jesus Christ, Tom. Could you just listen without jumping in with what you think for just one second?" Nick's voiced boomed louder than his laughter. And just for a second, both Nick and Tom stopped. It was unlike Nick to be so bold and demanding toward Tom. For some strange reason, Tom was the one person Nick let push him around – but not this time. Nick was a hero, and heroes commanded respect.

"Okay, okay. Please, enlighten me on your revelations," said Tom.

"Sam, the woman I've been obsessed with, and yes, I admit I had a bit of an obsession. A healthy obsession, not a creepy one. Well, not that an obsession can be truly healthy. After all it is an obsession. Sorry, I am getting off topic. The fact of the matter is, she talked to me, and not because she had to. She wanted to talk to me. For God's sake, she hugged me, and dare I say flirted with me. Tom, I want to be a hero. I am a hero. Let's do this right. Are you with me?"

Nick's rant left him out of breath and exhausted. However, as strange as it may have been, Nick enjoyed the feeling. He was filled with vigour and life and he wanted to run and shout from rooftops how happy and most of all how fulfilled he was. As he began to regain normalcy, his attention focused on Tom, who was simply sitting, silently, trying to take in everything he had just heard.

Nick was unsure of how Tom would react to his rant, he desperately hoped he was onboard. After all, every hero needs a sidekick.

11

THE STORY OF
FAMILY DINNERS

It was Tuesday, and Nick was off to his sister's home for the usual dinner. Nick was in a particularly upbeat mood having been celebrated for his heroics for the past few days. Nick assumed that over time he would get sick of it. After all, he hated people. The thought of them talking to him all day was exhausting. However, with each kind greeting or cheer, Nick felt uplifted. His very self-esteem catapulting to unfamiliar heights.

Nick walked along the sidewalk. He could see his sister's house getting closer. Tom had actually offered him a ride, but he had turned it down in order to capture the familiarity of his life before things changed. As he walked up to Kate's door, her neighbour stepped out of his.

"You must be Nick. I only just moved in a year ago. Still wild that we haven't met," the man said, as he walked toward Nick. Nick smiled politely, but there was something about this man that bothered him, and he could not figure it out for the life of him.

"Who are you?" said Nick, unsure of why he would know this man. As Nick stared at the man who was now about a meter away, Nick began to realize that his previous question might have come across as rude. For all he knew this was a fan of his. He must have heard about the incident and wanted to meet him in person, Nick thought. "My apologies, you caught me off guard. I meant to say, what is your name?" Nick stretched out his hand and shook the man's hand cheerfully.

"I'm Steve. I'm a friend of your sister's. Our children play together sometimes. Oh, and let me just say, your sister is a wonderful and kind woman."

Nick's jaw clenched as he swallowed hard. He could not help but feel uncomfortable. This was the infamous Steve- the man that his little sister was talking about. "Hello Steve, I've heard quite a bit about you," said Nick, his jaw still clenched tightly as the words struggled to leave his mouth.

"Really? I'm glad Kate mentioned me," said Steve with a smile. "I heard about the accident and I just wanted to say that I hope you are okay and what you did was very brave."

"Oh, just doing what any good man would do." Every ounce of Nick's body was tense. He wanted to end this conversation, but had no idea how to do so adequately. That is, he had no idea how to make Steve leave without seeming like an ass. Normally he would just coldly say that he had other things to do and depart. However, Tom told him that heroes need to be personable and friendly, and that his usual demeanor would lower his approval rating amongst fans. Nick was unsure what this meant, nor did he understand why he needed an approval rating, but nonetheless, he promised Tom that he would play-up this act.

"Well, I still think what you did was quite special. Kate is quite fond of you, you know. She talks about you quite a bit. I can see why," said Steve sincerely.

"Kate is just too kind." Nick stared back at Steve. He had nothing else to say to him. While Nick did not know him, he hated everything about him. He hated knowing that his sister spent time with this man. She ought to deserve better.

"Well, I'll let you go. Take care, Nick."

"You, too."

Nick did not turn around toward the door, but instead, waited for Steve to get into his car and drive off. Nick felt awkward running into his sister's home. While he wanted to escape from Steve, he definitely did not want his departure to look like an escape.

Nick opened the door to Kate's place and stepped in. No sooner was he greeted by his niece and nephew who once again threw their tiny arms around their uncle.

"Uncle, I'm glad you are okay," said Anthony.

"Please don't die, or get into any cars, or let any cars hit you," said Allison, as she squeezed him even tighter.

As Nick attempted to push his niece and nephew off of him, Kate came sprawling in, leaning in to hug him, although her hug was far less suffocating than her children's.

"Dinner is ready. Children, go wash up and let your uncle breathe for a moment," said Kate, shooing her children toward the bathroom. "Nick, you should wash up as well. Everything is already prepared so I'll be waiting for you all in the dining room. By the way, I am glad you are okay. You look good."

"Thanks, Tom has been getting me to present myself a little better. He said that a hero should carry themselves with some pride, so he had me update my wardrobe," said Nick, showing his tailor-made suit to Kate.

"I have no idea why you would need that, but I suppose if it makes you happy it makes me happy."

"I suppose it does," said Nick, looking down at his grey suit. It fitted him quite snugly. He could not help but feel that both the suit and he belonged in some sort of advertisement. You sknow, one of those hipster advertisements; where beautiful people wear beautiful clothes, and acoustic alternative songs play in the background just to add more ambiguity to the already confusing advertisement.

"Truthfully, I haven't completely figured out this hero thing yet;

but Tom seems to know what to do, so I'm just letting him take the reins on this one."

"I'm a little concerned with Tom having control of everything, but that's a discussion for later. We are here to enjoy a wonderful dinner, the four of us. So, go wash-up and get ready," said Kate, shooing Nick away from the kitchen.

Water flowed onto Nick's hands as his mind began to drift to memories of the past few days. For the first time in his life, Nick felt as if his life had purpose. Prior to this, Nick believed that life was meaningless, and that everything was simply a distraction to the nothingness that inevitably awaited all of us.

Nick walked into the dining room and sat down in his usual seat across from his sister – with his nephew and niece on either side of him. Despite this dinner being a usual occurrence, Nick could not help but feel anxious about it all, as if by sitting he was missing out on something important. Nick was sure that heroes didn't sit, they ran and flew. Nick wanted to embrace his new identity, and sitting idly did not seem quite right.

"Is everything okay, Nick?" asked Kate. Nick looked up toward his sister. Without even being aware of it, Nick was moving his food around with his fork, not eating, but just pushing it around. He stared for a moment, unsure of how to answer the question.

"Yeah, everything is great," said Nick, his gaze returning to his plate.

Kate's brow furrowed, as she was well aware when her brother was lying. However, she knew better than to call him out on the lie. Nick needed time, he needed to feel as if he could tell the truth on his own accord. And so, Kate decided to change the subject in order to lighten the mood. "So, why don't you tell me what Tom and you have planned? Tom always has some crazy plan, so it should be an interesting story."

"Tom's plan is not crazy, thank you very much." There was an obvious tone of annoyance as he said the words. Kate was not oblivious to this either. Kate was actually quite good at dealing with people. After all, she had to deal with her brother her entire life, so naturally she developed a strong sense of intuition.

"Nick, I didn't mean anything by it. I am not attacking Tom, nor you. I was just asking if you would be so kind to enlighten us on this plan of yours."

Nick resumed eye contact with his sister. His anxiousness began to fade. Perhaps his sister was capable of accepting his choices, he thought. In actuality, Kate never had a problem with Nick's choices, but rather, it was Tom's influence that bothered her more than anything. "Well, Tom had this brilliant idea to throw a party in my honour." A grin stretched across Nick's face just thinking about more people celebrating him.

"You're having a party?" asked Kate, shocked that this was the first she was hearing of this.

"Did you not hear what I just said? Tom is having the party, not me."

"I want to go to a party," said Anthony, who now seemed engaged in the conversation.

"Anthony, not now. I am trying to talk to your uncle," said Kate.

"You wouldn't want to go anyway," said Nick, looking at his nephew. "There will probably be alcohol, and scandalous women. Maybe drugs and prostitutes, I don't know. I have no idea what it might entail."

"Nick! Don't talk about that stuff at the dinner table! And why would you have that stuff at your party anyway?" questioned Kate, her frustration with her brother growing.

"I didn't say I wanted it. But Tom is planning it. I have no idea what he will do."

"And that's what scares me the most; that Tom is planning the bloody thing. You know, I'm sorry, I tried to hold my tongue, but I don't think that Tom taking charge in this situation is the best idea. Why don't you just take it slow, and not have lavish parties? I could throw you a *Glad You're Back Party* or maybe just a small get together with close friends and family. I have no idea why you need to be a 'celebrity'." Kate's eyes stared intently at her brother.

Nick's jaw clenched as he swallowed hard. Deep down, he was quite aware that his sister's intentions were pure. Kate had an incessant need to help, and that was something he loved about her. However, he hated when she tried to help him. He was not entirely sure why either. Nick was always stubborn, structured, and proud; but there was something more to it. Perhaps it was the fact that she was his little sister, or maybe it was the fact that he felt he had no control in his own life. Either way, Nick was not happy with his sister's advice.

"How about, I'll do what I want, and you do what you want," said Nick.

Kate did not say a word, nor did it seem as if she let out a breath. Nick stared across the table, but no one seemed to move. What frightened Nick even more was that he too was incapable of moving. It was as if time was frozen. Then, under her breath, Kate let out a reply that aggravated Nick more than she had ever done before. "Or maybe you'll just do what Tom wants."

Anthony looked up briefly. Despite his young age, he was aware of the tension. Anthony glanced toward his uncle, Nick's beady eyes seemed to be glaring at Kate's. Anthony quickly looked back down, instead opting to shuffle his vegetables around on his plate; his attempt to both try and ignore the high-tensioned situation and make it look like he had in fact eaten more vegetables than he had actually done.

"Uncle, your eye is twitching," said Allison, finally speaking up. Anthony gave her a swift kick from under the table. "Ow!" shouted Allison. It was clear that Allison had not clued in as quickly as Anthony. However, another swift quick from Anthony allowed Allison to see more clearly. Following her brother's lead, Allison began to shuffle her vegetables in a circle.

Time was no longer frozen. In fact, Kate's words had become a catalyst of chaos. Nick stood up. His very life decisions were under attack. Nick could not take her words idly. "Why the hell can't you just be happy for me?"

Kate's jaw dropped, shocked that her brother would ever speak to her like that. After all, in her mind she had been nothing but supportive and caring toward him.

"Kids, could you kindly go to your rooms, I need to talk to your uncle for a moment," said Kate, her eyes never deviating from their position on Nick.

"About time," mumbled Anthony. "I can only move my vegetables so much." Kate glared at Anthony.

Anthony and Allison quietly looked up, grabbed their plates and without another protest, left. Neither Kate nor Nick said a word. The two both stared intently at one another, with Nick's hands pressed against the table as if to keep him standing.

"Could you please sit down?"

"No, I'm not ready yet," replied Nick, surprised that he had chosen to take a stand on taking a seat.

"Well, I'd like to talk, but you standing there is making me nervous."

"I'll sit when I am ready." Nick waited for a moment in order to leave a sufficient time between his sister's request and his choice before finally taking a seat. This decision pleased both Kate and Nick, as both seemingly felt they had won the tussle against the other.

"Nick, I love you, you know that... I just feel that this celebrity thing is dangerous. Now, do not get me wrong, I'm very proud of you; but I also think that your kind deed will lose meaning amidst lights, cameras and parties. Most importantly, I'm afraid you'll lose something greater in the process... yourself."

Nick could not look at his sister while she spoke, because the rational side of him knew that what she was saying was right. Nick had never before been interested in the attention of others, nor did he ever need praise or glory. However, after being exposed to it all, Nick had no desire to go back. You see, attention and praise is a drug, and Nick had become an addict. One hit was not enough to quench his desire for purpose.

"Why can't you just be happy for me?" Nick's eyes welled up with emotion. Nick wanted this. No, he needed this. So, why was his sister so adamant that his heroics be hidden?

"I am happy for you, but I am also worried about you." Kate leaned forward in her seat, as if to try feel closer to her brother who was clearly hurting. Nick did not notice, nor did he reciprocate. He was hurt and he wanted her support, but at this point, he felt that he had already lost it.

"You're worried about me?" asked Nick, standing up once again. His voice boomed throughout the house. "You're worried about me, but you ought to worry about yourself."

"And what is that supposed to mean exactly?" asked Kate. While it was not in her character to yell, her voice had reached registers unfamiliar to even Nick.

"You know what it means," said Nick. Now, this was in fact a lie, because in all honesty, Nick had no idea what he meant by it. Kate was in control of her life. And despite how busy her schedule was, she always had time to help others. That being said, for Nick to rationalize all this would require Nick to use reason and logic, something he was incapable of doing at that time. All Nick could do was feel hurt. He needed her to understand that he was upset with her, and Nick knew no other way than to make her upset as well.

"Steve!" yelled Nick, as the name popped into his head. As Nick said the word it made him even more upset, which tricked him into believing that his anger was justified when in fact it was far from it. Instead, Nick had done what many people do when they are about to lose an argument — that is to pile on things that make both parties increasingly angrier, thus simultaneously prolonging and diverting the argument.

"My neighbour? What about him?" Kate's annoyance was growing exponentially. She had already discussed Steve before, and for Nick to bring him up now seemed to her, petty.

"Oh, come on. You spend all this time with another man that you know nothing about."

"Firstly, you make it seem like I see him every day, which is far from the truth. Secondly, he is my neighbour and his kid is friends with my kids, so it is only natural that I see him from time to time. Thirdly, I know quite a bit about him. He's a teacher, divorced because his wife cheated on him. He's very close to his father, not so much with his mother. He has a sister, who he loves dearly. Loves football. Plays the guitar. His favourite book is *1984*, and he is a good man." Kate's breathing was heavy, as she gasped for air just to finish off her little rant. Her knuckles had turned pale from her grasping the glass too tightly. Nick swore that if she held it any tighter the thing would shatter in her hands. Nick sat motionless. The only thing that seemed to be able to work at all was the beating of his heart. Forcing his body to work, Nick grabbed a napkin and wiped his mouth and hands. Too afraid to look his sister in the eyes, Nick kept his head down, staring at the fine china that resided on the table. The china looked awfully expensive. He was sure that Kate could not afford such things, but that was beside the point. He was not arguing with Kate over fine china. He was arguing with her over... Steve? No. Steve was his excuse to try and gain some points in his debate. He was arguing with her over his own life, and the fact of the matter was, she was winning. Nick was very aware that his sister had made many valid points, however, he desperately needed to redeem himself. After all, it was unlike Nick to just concede after a fight.

"Well, you seem to know an awful lot about him for spending so little time." Nick was sure to mumble the words, partly out of fear, but also on the slight chance she would not hear him which would allow him to rephrase it if necessary. However, Kate did not react. Her jaw clenched and her lips tight, she sat quietly, staring at her food. Nick needed her to react, and so he said the only thing he knew that would hurt her. "It's great to see you got over Ron so quickly."

And then there was silence. Everything stood still. Nick could not even hear his own thoughts. His mind seemed to be empty. Nick glanced over at Kate, her lips seemed to tremble, but apart from that, she was still.

There was never silence nor tension when Ron was around. Nick was sure that if anyone could have fixed the situation, it would have been Ron. He would have come into the room with his jovial face and wide smile and light up the room. He would not even have to say anything, although knowing Ron, he would. He would smooth the tension like soft butter over freshly baked bread. He might have even cracked a joke or two. That was the thing about Ron, he seemed to be good at everything. His way with words, and his ability to turn a phrase was something Nick always admired. However, there was no turning or smoothing anything anymore. Ron was not here. And by simply questioning Kate's love for him, he had created a moment that he had never thought possible.

Once she had finally gathered her will to speak, her voice was hallow and quiet, unlike Nick had ever heard before. "Nick, you're my brother and I love you, but get out."

Nick was still standing up, his arms firmly pressed against his sides. At first, he was sure that he had heard her wrong. As far as he was concerned, she meant get out as in, *get out of here* – a statement one would make if another were to say something farfetched. To Nick, it seemed very likely that his previous statement about his sister moving on from Ron may have crossed a line. So, Nick did what he thought was suitable – he sat down and did not say another word.

"Did you not hear me? Nick, I need you to leave!" Kate's eyes began to swell from the tears that were forming.

Nick looked up as he finally realized what she meant. He was being asked to leave. He had finally done it. He had crossed the line and pushed his own sister away. And it was all because of his ridiculous desire for fame and glory.

Nick stood up, wiped his mouth with a napkin, and pushed his chair in.

Kate had never kicked Nick out before. However, Nick supposed that there was a first for everything. He simply hoped that it would also be the last.

"Niiiiiiiiiiick..." The voice droned within his head again. This time, however, it did not ache, nor did it boom. This time it simply hummed, as an alarm clock would do. Nick pressed a finger to his temples, hoping the ringing would eventually disappear.

Kate stood up, confused by what was happening to her brother. Kate always knew that Nick was a bit strange, but this was strange, even by Nick's standards. She was still angry with her brother, but she would always care. Kate stood up, as she followed Nick toward the foyer.

"Is everything alright?" asked Kate. Her look of frustration had vanished, and instead, had been replaced with one of concern. Nick stared at her as the voice inside his head faded. He was still bitter and hurt by what he perceived was a lack of support from Kate. Of all people, he expected more from her. Alas, that was when Nick realized that we often expect more from the people we love.

Perhaps that is why we are so hurt when we feel they do not deliver.

"I'll be fine," said Nick coldly, as he picked up his jacket and headed out the door. Nick dared not turn around to see if she called him back. To do so was a sign of weakness, a defeat if you will. As the door closed behind him, Nick leaned his back against it and let out a sigh. He had just alienated the one person that had ever truly been there for him at least the only person still alive that cared genuinely.

Nick backed away from the door and turned around. It would be so easy for him to go back in and apologize. And the thing was that Kate would accept his apology. She was forgiving and understanding, even when she was hurt. Nick clasped the handle of the door. One turn was all he needed and things with his sister would be fixed; but of course doing so would mitigate his heroic dreams. Kate would never stand by as he embarked on this new life that had been thrust upon him. She was far too judgmental and orderly to ever allow something like that to happen. And so, Nick had a choice. To embrace his new life or to repair his old.

And that is when it hit him.

Nick released his grip of the handle and slowly made his way from the door. His new life was a dream, and to not embrace it was a disservice to all those too unfortunate to see their dreams realized. Nick could not go back.

12

THE STORY OF A WEDDING

The smell of rain was what Nick remembered best. It was a cool spring day, and the flowers were finally blooming. Ron always used to say he loved spring. He found the season to be full of optimism. Nick did not particularly care about the seasons, but somehow his friend had convinced him to share his point of view. Perhaps it was the way he spoke about it, or the way he acted when the weather began to warm up. All that Nick knew for sure was that Ron had a way of making even the simplest things seem inspiring.

It was about midday when the ceremony began. They had ventured quite far, as Kate insisted that while she did not want a big wedding, she did want to be married near a body of water. Kate, Ron, Nick and their parents ventured to the beach. Ron had discovered a cliff that seemed to perch it's way over the water, as if it was made for this very occasion.

There was no walk down an aisle, music, or even a maid-of-honour, or best-man. Just three people standing at the foot of a cliff. Kate wore a simple white dress that flowed out just above the knee. Ron wore slacks, a white t-shirt and a grey blazer. And Nick, well, Nick simply wore a dress-shirt and tie, as he stood stiffly in front the two lovers who held each other's hands.

Nick had managed to obtain a license to wed the two, something that both Ron and Kate insisted upon, given their desire for a more private and intimate ceremony.

"I am not one for speeches," said Nick, as he looked upon his sister and his best-friend. "However, I wrote one for the occasion. In the interest of saving time, and because I think the whole thing is cheesy, I am going to skip the traditional mumbo-jumbo of 'do you take this person in sickness and health', because let's be real, I know your answer."

"Just get on with it, Nick," said Ron, as both he and Kate looked at each other and chuckled.

"Right. Sorry. Okay, where was I? Oh, right, my speech." Nick reached into his front pocket and pulled out a ripped piece of paper that had clearly been the one and only draft of Nick's speech. "I have known Ron since I was a child, and well, I've known Kate all my life, because we're related... or so I've been told. I'm really not quite sure."

Kate glared at Nick who pretended not to notice, but then Ron let out a chuckle which led both Nick and Kate to follow suit.

"Maybe her parents can confirm the relation," said Ron, as he glanced over at Nick and Kate's parents who stood just off in the distance.

"We're related... unfortunately," said Kate, shaking her head. "Can we please continue? I'd like to be married now."

Nick shuffled through his cards, but in the corner of his eye, he could still see Ron smirking, which left him grinning.

"All I know is, I've never really believed in soul mates or in the idea of 'the one', but what makes the two of you really special is that you can make a pessimistic fool like me rethink things. This isn't to say that you both just somehow belong together, or that some cosmic entity brought the two of you together, but what matters is that you're both willing to work together. And that's the thing, really. At the end of the day, marriage isn't about finding that perfect person. It's about finding the person that you're willing to work with. And ever since the beginning, you two have never stopped working for and with one another. So, without further ado, do you two still want to do this thing?"

"Without a doubt," said Kate.

"Just try and stop me," said Ron.

At that moment, Nick saw Ron's magnetism and hopefulness very clearly as Ron held on to Kate's outstretched hands. It was very reminiscent of the first day the two friends met. Hope seemed to radiate off every part of Ron's body, and now, this hope was not just with him, but also with Kate. The two embraced, and Nick could swear that they both lit up. It was like looking at stars in a pitch-black sky. Ron had entered the lives of both Nick and Kate and had somehow managed to make their worlds brighter, more vivid, and most of all, hopeful. Perhaps it was the optimism with which Ron viewed the world, or maybe it was simply the way he made those around him feel? All that was certain was that Ron was a beacon of hope to those around him. If there was ever someone who deserved the title of a hero, it was Ron.

Then one day, the light went out. And so too did the hope that Nick once felt.

13

THE STORY OF SPOTLIGHTS

Nick threw on his jacket and tightened his tie. As he looked in the mirror, he turned his body in order to get a good look at himself from all angles. He looked quite dashing. While Nick believed that one should always dress in a presentable manner, he took extra care in his appearance that night.

It was the night of the infamous party that Tom had single-handedly orchestrated. There was a part of him that was absolutely terrified. His introverted nature rebelled at the idea of a big, lavish party with the centre of attention being none other than himself. But there was also a part of him that felt excited. There was a fire burning within him a desire to feel celebrated, accomplished, and most of all, loved. A party in his honour was sure to bring him these feelings at least that was what Tom told him.

Nick had not invited Kate to the party. As a matter of fact, Nick had not spoken to her since the night she told him to leave. Nick felt guilty about it all. He told himself that it was because he was still bitter about their argument. Truth be told, there was more to it. Nick had a new life, one in which his sister and her kids were not the focal point. For what he believed was the first time in his life, Nick had put himself first. He would take what he wanted, and do what he wanted to do, and there was no one to tell him otherwise. In fact, many of the people he had been talking to, who were mostly co-workers and fans of his heroics, had encouraged it.

Nick skipped down the stairs in an almost arrogant way. As he reached the bottom of the stairs, the front door swung open. Normally an intruder bursting through his door would startle Nick, but he was no sooner greeted by Tom wearing a tux with a bright red bowtie.

"Well, I'm glad to see you didn't over-dress," said Nick with a grin.

"My friend, the man of the hour." Tom raised his arms in the air, as if to beckon to Nick's glory. "You have to act the part if you're going to survive the cruelness that is the spotlight."

"If this spotlight is as cruel as you say, then why would I want to be in it?" responded Nick cheekily.

"Oh, it's a good cruel."

"A good cruel?"

"Yes, of course." Tom threw his arms in the air as if to point out the obvious. However, Nick still found it confusing on how anything cruel could be good. After all, cruelty seemed to be the antithesis of anything good, and so it was impossible for them to be related in any way.

"The spotlight is a lot like love. Cruel, torturous, and ever so demanding. But once you embrace it, you wonder how you ever lived in a world without it." Tom grinned, as if to await a reply.

"And what would you know about being in the spotlight?" laughed Nick.

"Nick, I've always been in the spotlight, I just never had an audience." Tom chuckled as he turned around and headed back toward the door. "Come on, the car is waiting."

As Nick stood at the foot of the steps, he could not help but admire Tom's wit. It was not something that he saw often, and so when it did occur, it made him feel proud. It may seem strange, but since the accident, Nick's perception of himself was directly influenced by those around him. Thus, if they were to act in a specific manner, that quality would then be reflected on him. Tom's wittiness was a reminder to Nick that he and his friends were both witty.

Nick walked out of his front door only to be greeted by the cold, bitter air. In fact, it was all he could think about. Now, had this occurred prior to his heroic transformation, Nick would have turned right around and called it a night. However, that was the old Nick. The new Nick had responsibilities and obligations. And of course, he could not miss a party in his honour. After all, to shun such flattery would be both rude and a direct hit to what was now an inflated ego.

A car beeped as Nick regained enough composure to look toward the driveway. There in front of him was not Tom's usual car. Instead, parked across his driveway was the largest SUV limo he had ever seen. With its tinted windows and black exterior, Nick assumed this was a vehicle made only for royalty or attention-starved celebrities. The car beeped once more and the rear window lowered. Tom peaked his head out as he shouted, "I'm sorry, was this not big enough for you?"

"No, actually I'm pretty sure I own one just like it."

"What? You do? Wait, no you don't."

It was quite apparent to Nick that Tom did not quite get his joke. Perhaps his earlier wittiness was simply a passing thing, like a comet. Yes, that was it. Tom was in fact a comet. For the longest time Nick had found it difficult to characterize his friend. But in that moment it had become quite clear that Tom was a comet. Tom was a rare occurrence, but when he was around it was always something special. That being said, Nick felt he owed it to Tom to explain his previous comment.

"It was a joke, Tom."

"Well, it's not very funny. Just get in, will you."

Nick trudged down his driveway to the door of the limo. At first he struggled to get in, simply due to the fact that the door stood level with his torso. After a few seconds of struggle, Nick managed to pull himself in, throwing his body across seats. Nick gazed across the room, its enormity overwhelmed him. The interior was massive, and yet, it was just Tom and himself inside.

"Do you think we'll have enough room?" asked Nick.

"Ha-ha — I get that one. Don't worry, old friend. You are a celebrity now. And being a celebrity requires you to carry yourself with some style. What better way than to arrive in a twenty-four person limo?"

"Well, aren't we, I don't know, twenty-two people short?" Nick asked.

"Hey, part of being a celebrity is doing things in excess. Like ordering more food and booze than one needs. Or arriving in a car that's clearly too large and gaudy for one person — or in this case, two."

Nick did not like his friend's logic and reasoning. It was the sort of thing that Nick hated. He could remember laughing and mocking such frivolous behaviour with Ron when he was around. Nick glanced down toward his watch. He continued to wear it despite the fact that it had not worked since the day of the accident. Nick could not get rid of it or even take the thing off. It was as if a part of him was bound to it; like Frodo to his ring — minus the fact that the ring was the embodiment of evil.

"I am not sure how I feel about this whole thing," said Nick. Nick still had reservations about his heroics and celebrity status, but somehow Tom always reassured him, and this time was no different.

"Nick, we are arriving in a limo that can fit twenty-four people. Granted there are only two of us, but you are forgetting one simple thing, my friend."

"And what is that?"

"You are forgetting that we may not be coming home alone."

Upon hearing this, Nick's mind immediately wandered to the thought of Sam. If she were to show up to the party, he could try to woo her. After all, she had made attempts at flattery and flirtation. Perhaps, this was his night. He could finally muster up the courage to do things properly and take her out. He had always felt awkward about not having a vehicle of his own to take women out, and now Tom had provided him with one big enough for every woman he had ever dated with twenty spots still open. And so, despite his previous reservations, Nick could not help but smile. In fact, Nick tried his best to contain his emotions, but at that very moment, it was as if he had lost complete control of all his emotions and so there upon his face a smile appeared and remained for the rest of the ride.

The limo pulled up to a hall not too far from where Nick worked. The place was small which surprised Nick. He had expected Tom to throw a large and lavish party, but by the looks of the place, it might be a far more intimate gathering, which was something Nick appreciated. Despite being located so close to his work, he had never been here before. Nick had not attended many parties, but it still surprised him that he never knew the hall even existed. As he entered through the archways, Nick could hear heavy electronic music, which he did not particularly like, along with the chattering of the guests. Nick was uncertain what to expect, and the idea made him incredibly nervous. Uncertainty was not something Nick was fond of.

"Are you ready?" asked Tom, as he swung the door open.

Nick took a deep breath, closed his eyes, and then reopened them. As he took a step forth, it was as if he was entering a separate realm of existence. He had gone through the figurative wardrobe, and what he saw amazed him. The ceiling was arched and raised high above them. It was so high that he could not tell where the wall ended and the ceiling began. Nick raised his head to take it all in. Small white lights covered them like a blanket of stars. As Nick walked further, he noticed a stage in the back, a bar to the left, and there in the centre stood a statue of him in herculean fashion with his arms raised and pushing back a car.

"How the hell did you pull all of this off?" asked Nick, turning toward Tom.

"I have my ways. And by ways I mean that I agreed for you to do a commercial for a Japanese game show."

"Are you serious?"

"No," laughed Tom, rolling his eyes. "See, I can make jokes too."

This was not something Nick found particularly funny. To arrange plans without his knowledge was criminal. Nick liked control; he needed control. To lose it would in fact undo his very character; but his character was changing. Nick was more open and willing to let others take charge and he had promised Tom complete control over his new heroic life.

"So, what do I have to do to pay for all of this?"

"Nothing."

"Nothing?" questioned Nick, unsure of whether he had heard it wrong.

"Most of this stuff was donated by various businesses and the media. There are cameras documenting the whole thing," said Tom, pointing to various cameras around the room.

"Okay, so I don't have to do anything for this?"

"Nothing at all. Just enjoy," said Tom, as he picked up two cocktails from a waitress that walked by, taking a sip of one before handing the other to Nick.

Nick took a sip of the orange concoction that had been placed in his hands. Nick had never been a big drinker, but upon taking a sip, he was immediately swept away.

"This is absolutely delicious," said Nick, taking another gulp of the drink.

"Here, take another." At this point, Tom seemed to be grabbing the drinks from thin air. However, Nick did not hesitate to accept.

"Well, why don't we go mingle?"

"With whom?" asked Nick, temporarily removing his lips from his glass.

In what seemed like a flash, two women who were quite beautiful, appeared before them. Just like the drinks, Tom managed to make these beautiful women appear from nothing. The woman to the right of Nick wore a little black dress that seemed to be painted on her body. Her luscious brown hair cascaded down to her shoulders, like waves hitting the shore. The woman to Nick's left wore a similar dress, but in red. Her hair, however, was a pale blond, and was straight as a needle. Her thin bangs draped over her forehead, which only drew attention to her pale-blue eyes.

"Ladies, are you having a good time?" asked Tom, temporarily placing his hand on one of the women's shoulders.

"Oh yeah, it's a blast!" said one of the ladies, who appeared to be already heavily intoxicated.

Nick did not know either of these women. As a matter of fact, he had never seen them before. Nick began to wonder why they were even here. As Nick looked around the room, he began to realize that he, in fact, knew very few people in attendance.

In an attempt to make Tom aware of his query Nick whispered, "Tom, who are these women?" However, due to the loud music and the fact that he was slightly inebriated, his attempt to whisper became more of an awkward shout that both women clearly heard. And so, for a few seconds there was an awkward stare down between the two women, Nick and Tom.

"Who cares   they're hot," whispered Tom.

While Nick was very much aware that the women were 'hot', he could not help but wonder why they would show up to a party where they did not even know the host. Nick thought it best to ask them, partly out of curiosity but also because he thought it might be a good conversation starter.

"So, why are you here?" asked Nick. While his intentions were pure, his phrasing came off both cold and slightly hostile. To say the least, the women were not impressed. They began to stare at Nick, as if he were a leper.

Tom tugged on his arm pulling him away from the two women. "Excuse me, ladies, just one moment," said Tom, pulling Nick into a huddle, as if they were part of a team devising a strategy for their opposition. "What are you doing?" asked Tom, shaking his head.

"I was trying to talk to the women like you wanted."

"That's not talking! That's an interrogation!"

"Well, neither of us are talking to them, and I am fairly certain they can hear you," said Nick, as if suddenly becoming completely aware of social etiquette.

"Oh, bugger off! Just leave it to me and maybe we'll both get laid."

Nick was slightly taken aback by Tom's hostility toward him. Tom knew that Nick was awkward around the opposite sex, so it should have come as no surprise that he would be terrible in any social interaction. Nick began to feel that Tom's judgement was a bit selfish. Nonetheless, Nick carried forth, obeying Tom's orders both willingly and blindly.

"Ladies, I am sorry for the interruption. My friend Nick and I were just discussing his heroic story. This is actually his party."

The two women looked at each other, a grin slowly stretching across both faces. As the grin finally turned into a smile, both women simultaneously looked toward Nick and Tom who were both standing, awaiting a response.

"You're THE Nick?" asked the brunette.

"Well, I am A Nick. I guess by THE, you are referring to the party and the statue," Nick pointed to the statue, hoping not to seem too braggadocios. Nick was having a difficult time speaking, mainly because he was struggling to make eye-contact. It seemed to Nick that every time his eyes met with either of the women, it became an awkward affair; that is, the women were staring in an alluring way. It was as if they were not really looking at him, but sizing him up, like how a predator would size its prey. Nick continued to ramble until Tom nudged him in his side and handed him another drink. This seemed to do the trick, because Nick began to feel a little more relaxed.

"Yes, the day I saved that woman is still a bit of a blur. I remember seeing the woman in front of me and then in the corner of my eye I saw the car coming, and I didn't think, but reacted. It was like I knew what I had to do before I even did it."

Everyone went silent.

"You're... so brave," uttered the blond-haired woman, her hand gently rubbing Nick's shoulder, as if to soothe the ailing hero.

"That's my buddy Nick. He's the bravest man I know. I just..." said Tom, as he began to pretend to choke up. As he did this, the other woman put her arms around Tom, consoling the loyal sidekick. "I just wish I could do half the good that this man does every day."

Nick grinned, shrugged his shoulders and patted his friend on the back. As he did this, Tom pulled him in for a hug and whispered in his ear. "We are so close to getting these women to come home with us - keep it up." Nick began to pull away, but before he was able to release himself from the iron-clad grip of Tom's hug, his eyes caught a glimpse of heaven, and there was no turning back. There across the room stood Sam. Her elegant and sleek black dress showed off

97

everything that was beautiful about her, yet left enough mystery to entice the eyes of all those within her vicinity. Her dark brown hair was pulled back into a bun, and her piercing green eyes seemed to brighten the room far more than any of the lights within the hall. Nick was utterly captivated.

Nick pulled away from Tom, refusing to break his gaze away from Sam. It seemed at that moment, she too noticed him. The two stood still, staring at one another, neither moving, save the beating of their hearts and the exhalation of their breath.

Sam and Nick were frozen, both waiting on the other to take a step forward. The moment was eventually broken by the drunken blonde throwing her arms around Nick. Nick jumped back at first, startled by the contact.

"Is everything okay, hun?"

Refusing to acknowledge her, Nick gently removed her arms from around him. His eyes continued to remain fixed upon Sam too afraid to break focus, as if doing so would undo the very reality of the moment.

Now, jealousy is an interesting thing. It often appears when the very things we take for granted are threatened. The blonde-haired woman threatened Sam, as they both vied for Nick's attention. And so, as a woman determined and driven, Sam strode toward Nick.

"I am sorry, but... I... I... have somewhere else to be," said Nick.

"Where are you going, Nick? This is a sure thing," said Tom, as he attempted to pull his friend back to his direction. Nick would not have any of it. The fact of the matter was, he did not want a sure thing. He wanted Sam. He had had his heart set on her from the moment he saw her, and so all other things became secondary to Nick.

Nick walked with great pace and purpose across the room. Despite the crowd, they did not seem to get in his way; rather, it felt as if the people danced out of his way. It felt as if they moved to make way for the inevitable, the coming together of these two people.

"Hi," said Nick.
"Hello," replied Sam.

"I am so happy." The words fumbled out of his lips. Regardless of the scenario, Nick always seemed to struggle to speak to Sam. This time, however, he managed to do something he had previously never been able to do — he was able to recover. "That is to say, I am happy you are here."

"Well, I am equally happy. That is to say, I am equally happy to be here... with you." Sam reached out her hand and grabbed his. Her touch was smooth, yet forceful, as if to say, *"I know what I want."* And it became quite clear to Nick that she wanted him. Little did she know, that he had always been hers.

"I know it seems rash, but the night is young, and I don't really care about any of this. Would you like to get out of here? Maybe grab a coffee, or a bite to eat? Or maybe both? It doesn't matter. I just would like to take you somewhere other than here."

"What about all the cameras, don't you want to take some pictures together, maybe do an interview or something? After all, aren't we all here for that?" Sam pulled him closer. Nick could feel her heart beat against his chest. Her breath against his neck gave him shivers. He was completely and undeniably at her will.

"You want pictures, you got it." Without hesitation, or even a thought, Nick grabbed the first camera he saw – which happened to belong to a journalist from Buzzfeed or Complex — one of those online magazines. "Will this do?" Nick smiled at Sam, holding the camera up, as if to display it as a trophy.

"It's a start," replied Sam with a smirk.

Nick held the camera out with his right hand as he edged closer to Sam. As Nick began positioning the camera, making sure to get a good angle, he could feel Sam's arms around him. His body tensed at her touch, but then interestingly enough, he began to relax. It reminded Nick of home. He felt both free and secure. He stretched his arm around her waist gently, but Sam seemed to squeeze against it, as if she wanted him to hold her tighter. Nick juggled the camera awkwardly, but managed to click the button as the flash brightened everything around them. As he turned the camera around to view what was now an immortalized moment, he was both shocked and confused by what he saw. Sam's face was blurred out completely, but his was not. In fact it was just her face. The rest of the image seemed quite clear.

"Oh, could I see it?" asked Sam, reaching out toward the camera.

"Ah, I don't think it turned out right. Let me just get this fellow to take the picture." Nick passed the camera back to the journalist, who did not seem happy that his camera was abruptly taken.

"Could you take a picture of us?"

The man reluctantly nodded. Nick resumed his pose, this time, holding on to Sam even tighter, pulling her right against his body. It was clear that she did not mind, as she pressed against him, as if to mark her territory. The flash went off and their pose withered as the two of them relaxed their grips. Nick reached out to grab the camera, but the journalist refused to part with his possession again.

"If you want to see it, you can come over here," said the journalist.

Nick and Sam smiled at one another before moving forth toward the camera. The journalist turned the camera around so the two of them could have a look at their second attempt of immortalization.

"Oh, we look absolutely fabulous," said Sam, as she tugged on Nick's arm.

Nick stared at the photo, but once more noticed that Sam's face was completely blurred out. In truth it looked faded, as if the camera was the lens in which one views a dream.

"What about the blurred out face?" asked Nick.

"What do you mean?" said Sam. "Our faces look fine."

"Well, mine does, but yours doesn't." It took a second for Nick to realize that his words may have come across as a bit cruel, and that perhaps his analysis of the photo required more clarification than what he had given. "What I mean is, your face looks blurred out. You don't see that?" Nick pointed at the camera screen, but as he did, the journalist pulled the camera back.

"Do not touch the camera!"

"I'm sorry." Nick jumped back. "But look at the picture, her face is blurred out."

The journalist looked at the picture for a moment and then turned the screen back toward Nick and Sam. "It looks fine to me."

"What are you talking about? Her face is completely blurred out. What kind of photographer are you?" His frustration began to increase exponentially. It was clear to him that the picture was blurred, strangely just on Sam's face. However, everyone, including the photographer, seemed blind to it. This bothered Nick tremendously. Nick hated when others failed to recognize something so obvious.

"Nick, the face isn't blurred. It's fine, just leave it alone."

The journalist stormed off, and Nick turned away as well, as the mere sight of the journalist would only reawaken his frustration. "I still don't understand how none of you could see that it was blurred." Nick looked toward Sam who seemed to be getting annoyed by his obsession with being right. "Okay, let's forget about that. Let's get out of here."

As Sam opened her mouth to reply, all eyes turned toward a voice coming from the stage. "Hello, and how is everyone doing tonight?" shouted the man on the stage. The entire room began to cheer, clap and make other various noises of excitement. Nick never understood the point of crowds and cheering. To Nick, they were all sheep, chanting about things they truly did not care about, if only to feel as if they are part of something, even if it was just for a moment. That being said, what confused Nick even more was the man on the stage.

"Who is that?" Nick questioned aloud. However, no one around was paying any attention to Nick's confusion.

"I'm Milo, and I'll be your MC for the night," said the man on the stage. He wore a fitted white tux, and had a high-top fade. Here was a man who was clearly out to get attention. "Before we really get crazy and wild tonight, we have to give a big shout out to the man of the hour. Nick, get up here and say a few words."

Nick stood absolutely still, he had not planned a speech, nor did he even like public speaking. This was not part of the agenda. The crowd began to holler as all eyes gazed upon him. Nick felt like a creature in a zoo, a spectacle for all to see.

"Go up there," said Sam, nudging his arm.

Nick had no intention of speaking, for all he cared he could just leave and never look back However, Sam's insistence seemed to have a great influence on him, because before he knew it, he was standing on stage, staring down at the crowd below. They continued to cheer and Nick continued to hate every minute of it. This moment could not be real, it felt more like a nightmare. All that was left was for him to be naked and he would know that it was just a dream. Nick's eyes scanned the room, looking for something to say. It took him only a few seconds, but what felt like minutes to focus in on two very important things. One was Sam, standing there smiling at him. Her smile was bright, and Nick found courage in her. The second was surprisingly the gaudy statue of himself. There was something about the image of himself performing the heroic deed that inspired him. And although he knew that all of it was a lie, and nothing about his heroics were true, looking at the statue and then toward Sam made him believe that maybe he was a hero. That maybe, his perceived heroics were an inevitable part of his destiny. This very idea sparked a madness with him.

"Hello, or... good evening... either way, salutations."

The crowd stood silently. It became quite clear to Nick that this crowd was a reflection of himself. How could he expect to inspire, motivate or excite anyone if he himself lacked all those qualities? In fact, all people are essentially mirrors of one another. Thus, it is quite easy to understand or influence another, all one must do is first understand themselves.

"I beg of you to pardon my awkwardness, I am not one to speak in front of so many incredible people."

A few chuckles could be heard amidst the crowd. Ah, flattery, the one thing that grabs anyone's attention. Nick felt rather proud and delighted by the laughter. It invigorated him in a way that surprised him. Like Tinkerbell to applause, he began to live for the laughter.

"Let me first start of by saying that yes, I am a hero."

The crowd cheered as those in the audience began to clap and howl with delight. The man of the hour had proclaimed his greatness before them. Like the coronation of a King, these people were bearing witness to the birth of greatness. Amidst the dense crowd, every soul believed that Nick was a hero. However, no one believed it more than Nick himself.

"But I am also just a man — flesh and blood like anyone else here. I did what anyone with a heart would do if faced with the same decision. That is, I chose another over myself. You see, self-sacrifice is often looked down upon. Perhaps this is due to the negative connotation attached to the word *sacrifice*, but rest assured, sacrifice bears no negativity. Sacrifice is in fact a necessary component in our humanity. If you think for a moment, where would we be without sacrifice? Without the sacrifice of our soldiers, we may not have freedom. Without the sacrifice of our officers we may not have security. Without the sacrifice of our teachers, we may not have knowledge. Without the sacrifice of our parents or caregivers we may not have been here at all. So, I ask you, am I a hero? Yes, but not because I beat death, but because I chose to sacrifice myself for another. I am more than just a hero. I am your hero!"

As the last words left Nick's lips, he was filled with a strange euphoric energy. The crowd erupted with deafening cries of approval. Nick had done it. He had immortalized himself. He had placed his stake in history — albeit local history, but history nonetheless. Nick had always longed for some sort of purpose in life, and it had become clearest then. He embraced the approval of his adoring fans, smiling and waving, blowing kisses to everyone around him. If this was a dream, Nick was sure that he never wanted to wake up.

While Nick basked in his glory, there was a smile he had briefly forgotten about. There in the centre of the room stood the woman who had been waiting for him – Sam. She cheered and hollered just as loud as the rest of them. The crowd was beautiful, majestic, but to Nick, nothing not even the immortalization of his heroics compared to the brightness of Sam's smile. At that moment, all Nick wanted to do was grab a cup of coffee with the woman in waiting.

14

THE STORY OF

COFFEE, TEA, AND TESTIMONIES

Nick had managed to sneak out of his own party — which was no easy task as nearly every Tom, Dick, and Harry wanted to shake his hand and speak to him about something that Nick clearly had no interest in. However, Nick played the part. After all, what is a hero if not empathetic? Sam did not seem interested in leaving. She insisted on numerous occasions that she wished to be interviewed by various journalists and Nick was quite oblivious to Sam's protests. There was only one thing on his mind, and that was to spend some time alone with her. He did not care what they did, or if they even did anything at all. What mattered most to Nick was that they be together — even for just a moment. Eventually she obliged, after Nick promised to accompany her to an interview for a magazine — which Nick had never heard about, but according to

Sam it was very popular amongst women aged sixteen to twenty-nine. How Sam knew the statistic so readily, Nick did not bother to ask. He trusted her knowledge and her judgement. Truthfully, it only enticed Nick to her even more, for it showed him that Sam had interests.

"So, I'm really glad we got to finally sneak out of there. Not that I wasn't having fun, but it's kind of nice just to have a real, deep conversation with someone, you know?"

"Yes, totally," said Sam.

"So, I thought we could grab a tea or coffee, and just talk, maybe get to know each other better. Is that okay?"

"Yeah, of course."

The words delighted Nick to the very core. He had not been on a date for quite some time, let alone been interested in anyone as much as he was interested in Sam. This would be their first date, and hopefully, one of many. Perhaps it was all too soon to plan the future, but Nick could not help wonder where their relationship might lead. This was all very strange to Nick. Not because it was a first date, nor because he barely knew her, but it was strange because it was not in his nature to do so. Nick was a practical, pragmatic man. He did not bother with ideas, and the future. As Nick pondered his future with Sam, he did in fact remind himself of his nature — that he was a man concerned with real things, or at the very least, things that concerned only him. He was not the sort to let emotions dictate his present. He was a man in charge of his environment. But then, he looked at her and felt something that he had never quite felt before. She felt real. She was the most real thing he had ever known. Nick was no longer in charge of his environment – Sam was. And for all he cared, she could bend his reality to her will.

"Just one question," added Sam.

"Yes, anything."

"When will the interview with the magazine take place?"

Nick looked at the ground, moving a rock back a forth between his feet. He could not dare look at Sam in her eyes. He had hoped that their time together would be special, and not consist of idle talk of frivolous things.

The wind blew, chilling Nick to the very core. He could feel the air shifting around them, and it was not long before his thoughts followed suit. Just as easy as it was for Nick to be consumed by feelings of love and grandeur, so too was he susceptible to feelings of betrayal. Now, it may seem extreme to classify Sam's questions as an act of betrayal, but to Nick, there was no denying the intention of her words. Like Brutus to his Caesar, he had been hurt by the person he trusted most. There seemed to be no other way for him to look at it. Here he was, enchanted by the woman of his dreams, and her biggest concern was her own self-promotion. While Nick contemplated how he should handle the situation, Sam continued to speak.

"I really want to make sure I look my best. Are you going to introduce me as your girlfriend? We really should get our story straight. How should we say we met? We need something interesting. Oh, maybe I was in a terrible loveless relationship, and you swept me off my feet and convinced me that I deserved better? Actually, that makes me sound a bit slutty. Perhaps we met while vacationing in Paris. You were writing at a local coffee shop and I dropped my purse with all of my credit cards and information. You tracked me down and returned it to me, and ever since, we've been madly in love? Yes, I think I like that one. What do you think?"

Nick was unable to comprehend, let alone hear the ramblings of Sam. Not because he did not want to listen, but rather, every ounce of him was replaying a single moment. *Are you going to introduce me as your girlfriend?*

The words seeped through him like venom. All that he previously thought vanished with the dying of the wind. No longer did he feel cold or hurt, but rather, he felt warm and loved. There was not a doubt in his mind that he would allow Sam to call him *boyfriend*. It, after all, was the point of his hero's journey. His identity as a celebrity hinged on the possibility of a love affair between Sam and himself.

"We're here," said Sam

THIS IS THE STORY OF NICK.

Nick looked up to see the coffee shop sign above him. He was completely unaware that he had even taken a single step out of the hall, let alone travelled to a coffee shop. In fact, it all felt quite surreal, as if the hall had transformed into the coffee shop, like a cut in a film. Nick slowly transferred his gaze away from the sign and back toward Sam. Her green eyes shimmered, drawing him in with every blink. Her dark-brown hair seemed to fall effortlessly on her shoulders, and her porcelain skin shimmered in the moonlight. How something could be so beautiful, Nick did not know. Nick slowly moved in closer, hoping to close the distance between their two bodies. However, no matter how close he moved in, it almost seemed as if she was just out of reach. Nick stretched out his hand and managed to place it around her waist. Sam did not shy away from the embrace. Instead, Sam let a sly smirk break through her tightly-bound lips. Nick had the fortune of seeing the smile he was now all too familiar with. Yet, to Nick, it was just as special as the first time. Sam moved in closer as she tilted her head, awaiting the inevitable kiss from her hero. This was it. Nick lowered his head, mirroring the tilt of his partner. As they both held one another, their movements seemed rhythmic and effortless. This was more than just an embrace, it was a dance. Nick pressed his body against Sam's. He could not feel her heart, but the way his raced, he was sure that she felt his. In fact, his heart was racing tremendously, so much so that it began to actually physically hurt. Nick slowly pulled away, pushing his body away from Sam's.

"What's the matter?" asked Sam.

Nick had no response, because he, in fact, had no idea what was wrong. The pain worsened. Nick clenched his heart, hoping that by some miracle, he could stop whatever was happening to him. It was then that Nick felt it. A jolt of electricity surging through his body. Nick screamed out in pain and just for a moment, everything went white.

Nick fell to the ground, as his limp body lay outside the coffee shop. Sam stood over his body, like a mourner at a funeral. Nick was not dead, but to Sam, he might as well have been. She screamed hysterically, quickly turning in a circle to see if there was anyone around to help.

"Oh my God, I think I killed him," thought Sam. Sam, in fact had not killed him, but it was only natural for her or anyone to assume that she had something to do with his fit. After all, they had only just embraced when Nick wriggled with pain and lost consciousness.

Her panic, however, did not last long. With another surge in his chest, Nick arose. "Hey, why was I on the floor?"

Sam looked in terror, as if she was witnessing the rising of the dead. There in front of her was not the Nick she had left the party with. To her, this was a creature of the undead. Not a hero, but a monster.

"Sam, what happened to me? I remember feeling a pain in my chest, and then... everything went white."

Nick held his chest, and as he did, he once again became familiar with the pain. However, this time it did not physically hurt, but rather, it was as if he was remembering the pain. Nick gazed upon his chest, like a mystery he could not solve. Nick slowly diverted his attention back toward Sam who was still standing motionless. She, too was a mystery, albeit a different and more complicated one.

"Sam?"

The street was completely empty save the two bodies who once yearned for one another. However, there was no longer any yearning... there was just waiting. Nick looked at the coffee shop next to him, hoping that his gesture might entice Sam to continue with their date. However, upon glancing at the shop, the lights were off, and the people within were no longer there. Staring into the little Parisian-esque coffee shop, Nick felt an empty, sinking feeling.

Nick looked desperately into Sam's green eyes. This time, however, he was not drawn into them. This time they seemed to be pushing him away with every blink. Nick was losing her. He did not know why, but he knew that despite her physical immobility, she was leaving. Nick thought that perhaps if he tried to explain, maybe communicate to her what had just happened, she might understand. Maybe, just maybe, she was frightened, and all he needed to do was reassure her that he was in fact okay. This hero had not fallen, it was simply a temporary stumble.

"Sam, I'm okay," said Nick, as he stood up, dusting off his clothes.

"I think I just had some bad cocktails, I'm okay, I swear."

Sam did not reply, nor did her mood waiver. Nothing he said had changed anything. If Nick was to win her back, he needed to do more. Nick pondered a way to reach out to her. After all, there must be a way, there always is. No human is completely immune to logic and reason. Of course Nick realized that emotion was a powerful tool, but he was sure that rational thought could prevail amongst even the stoutest of emotional barriers. Sam had barricaded herself in fear, but Nick would rescue her, this was his hero's duty.

"I really think that I just had a little too much to drink. I'm sorry, I shouldn't have. It really isn't like me. Please, let's just forget that it happened, and continue this date."

"What happened? That wasn't alcohol! I don't know what it was, but it wasn't alcohol. And as for our date, I don't think so. This... this isn't going to work."

"Alright, no, I understand. What happened was kind of scary. How about I just take you home and we can reschedule. It's been a long night anyway. We can try this again once we get some rest."

"Nick, I don't think you understand what I am saying. I'm not saying this date isn't going to work... I am saying that we're not going to work."

The conversation had taken a nasty twist. Whatever had happened to Nick, scared Sam. This fear, however, did not stem from concern, but from Nick himself. Sam was not adequately equipped with the emotional nor practical skills to figure out Nick or his issues. In a moment of complete transference, the very moods of these two people had changed. Nick was no longer governed by logic and reason, but emotion. Now, being governed by one's emotions is not a bad thing by any means. In fact, those governed by emotions tend to be empathetic and understanding. They choose people over things, and this is a noble cause. But Nick was not governed by these positive things. Nick was only governed by fear, despair, and desperation.

"But, Sam, what about the interview? I thought you wanted to do the interview. Think about all the great things that can come with it. Just stick with me, please. I promise I'll give you all that I can."

"I'm sorry, but it's not worth it. I thought it would be easier to make this work, but it's not. I... I can't be that kind of person." Sam's voice cracked as she said each word.

"What kind of person?" Nick's entire body began to shake. He could feel his eyes welling up, and once again, his heart was racing. However, this time, his heart was racing not from physical pain, but by an emotional one.

"I just... I can't."

And then she was gone. Just like that, she disappeared into the darkness of the night. It was as though the entire affair subsided as quickly as the excitement had. There, all alone, stood Nick. He watched blankly at the space in which she formerly stood. A part of him hoped that perhaps, through some divine intervention, she would reappear, this time not with fear but hope. Nick clung to this idea just as he had clung to his desire for her all those years. However, as strong as his will for her was, it was not strong enough for her to reappear. Nick may have convinced himself that he was a hero, but he certainly was no superhero.

So he stood, alone in the street. No longer was Sam the girl in waiting. The only one waiting was him. Nick had not been on many first dates, but as far as first dates were concerned, he was sure this was by far the worst.

15

THE STORY OF BROKEN LIGHTS AND BROKEN HEARTS

Nick sat in the living room at Kate and Ron's place. They had just bought their first home and they wanted to celebrate. Normally, Nick did not like celebrations, but he did believe that owning a home was a practical and necessary feat. And so, he willingly came over to their house, with a bottle of wine in hand. Nick did not like wine too much, but he felt that it was courteous to bring a gift for such an occasion. Wine seemed like the best choice, simply because he noticed that others seemed to enjoy it.

Kate sat on the floor watching her children play. Anthony had recently turned five and Allison was three. Nick really did not like them at this age. He found children as a whole to be quite annoying, but young children were the worst. You see, Nick felt that young children lack both logic and empathy, the two things that make

111

anyone a decent person. By his standards, his niece and nephew were horrible people he was forced to love because they were related. Despite this, he occasionally found enjoyment with the little buggers. On this night specifically, he was playing a board game with the children Monopoly. Nick felt that one was never too young to learn Monopoly.

"Oh, Anthony. You landed on my hotel, but you don't have enough money to pay. So here's what I'm going to do. All the property you own is now mine, and now you're bankrupt. Which means you are poor and out of the game," said Nick.

"Wait, so I can't play? Why?"

"I just told you. You landed on my property, and you don't have enough money to pay."

"You can have my money, Anthony," said Allison handing over the very little she had left."

"No handouts, Allison. Your brother has to learn," said Nick.

"I hate this game," said Anthony gloomily.

"Monopoly is a wonderful game, you just need to learn," said Nick, as he counted his money. "By the way, when's dinner? I'm starving."

Nick looked toward Kate. Her leg was shaking, and every few seconds, she glanced up toward the clock, as if she was waiting on something.

"I know you're hungry, Nick. We'll have dinner soon. Ron got caught up at the office, and he said he might be a little late." As Kate said the words, Nick could hear concern in her voice, because Ron, just like Nick, was chronically early for everything.

Nick looked at his watch, and then looked back at his sister who resumed her games with the children. Ron was more than a little late, he should have been home an hour ago. Just as the thought entered Nick's mind, the phone rang. Kate looked up toward Nick, who stared right back at her. Kate quickly stood-up and headed toward the phone.

"Hello, how may I help you? Yes, this is she, who am I speaking with? Pardon? Is he okay!?"

Nick's heart began to race as he stared toward his sister. Her left hand was balled into a fist, and her eyes were swelling. Nick hoped that whatever was happening on the other side had nothing to do with Ron, however, a sinking feeling inside told him that his fears were a reality. The phone crashed to the floor, and soon after, Kate followed suit. Nick rushed over, throwing his arms around his sister, her head resting against his chest. Kate wept profusely, and all Nick could do was sit silently and hold her. He did not need to hear what happened, because somehow, he knew.

Hope, as it turned out, was an entity that was only present as long as the person that embodied it.

16

THE STORY OF VOICES

The street was quite dark, only a few small street lights illuminated the path in front of him. Nick was without the limo that Tom had ordered, and he was far too embarrassed to call him at a time like this. Of course this is a silly thought, as Nick deemed Tom a friend, a best-friend, in fact. And a friend, regardless if they are deemed to be the best, is always understanding and supportive. Otherwise, why call them a friend at all?

At this point, Nick did not want a friend. He wanted to be alone. His only desire, Sam, had left him just as quickly as she arrived. Nick thought about calling Kate, as he knew she would be there in an instant; but Nick could not bring himself to do so. All Nick could remember was how badly he had treated Kate the last time he had gone for dinner. Plus, Nick had not invited Kate to the party and thus calling her would require him to explain the entire situation to her. That explanation alone was a greater embarrassment than anything Nick was feeling in his current state. There was no point in adding more misery to his already miserable night.

While Nick walked along the sidewalk, moving ever closer to his little duplex, it became quite clear to him that he was not alone. Inside his head, he could hear the droning of the familiar voice. *Niiiiiiiiickkkkk.* The voice repeated, over and over again. Normally the voice lasted a few seconds and then ceased, but this time it did no such thing. The voice continued to repeat his name, much to his annoyance. Nick hated the voice. While he had become accustomed to it, the very fact that he was hearing it made him uneasy. He did not like to think of himself as crazy, but he knew that hearing voices was never a good thing.

Nick trudged along, his journey home seemingly never-ending. Nick tried his best to ignore the voices, but they seemed to get louder with each passing minute. Nick placed his hands in his pocket, hoping to find an answer to his problems. Nick firmly believed in putting things that he might need in his pockets. It gave him comfort to know that at all times, there was something he could use inside his pockets.

As Nick reached into his pocket, he could not find anything useful. This was the problem with formal attire: It offered very little room for relevant things. Nick continued to scramble, searching frantically in every pocket for something to soothe his pain. Then he felt it. There in his front jacket pocket laid his ear buds. He excitedly placed them into his phone and then stuck each bud into the corresponding ear. If Nick could not ignore the voice, he would drown it out with music. While Nick cared about reality, he also needed to escape it from time-to-time. He had done it countless times before, so that night, when he needed it most, should not be any different.

Nick scrolled through his phone, searching for a song to set the mood. Perhaps it was the current state of his despair, or maybe it was the voice echoing in his head, but he could not for the life of him find a suitable song. And so, he decided to let fate decide as he clicked randomize on his phone. The beat kicked in, and right away

Nick knew the song. Alicia Key's *Try Sleeping with a Broken Heart* played. "How appropriate," thought Nick. Of all the songs he had, fate decided to remind him of how badly his heart hurt. It did not matter though. Nick was determined to get lost in the music and change his reality in any way that he could.

The song continued to play, as Nick closed his eyes and took it all in. He walked slowly down the sidewalk, and there was not a sound nor a single soul this night. As the chorus kicked in, so did Nick's speed. He opened his eyes and looked around, expecting the world to change to his liking. However, to his disbelief, everything was exactly as it was. "Perhaps, I'm just not embracing the music enough," he thought.

Nick began to move and sway, his walking speed quickening to that of a jog. Despite his best efforts, nothing changed. The world remained, and the voice inside his head just got louder. Nick began to sprint, hoping that he could outrun the voice, or at the very least, get home sooner. However, with every step that he took, the voices became louder. And so, to combat against it, Nick increased the volume of his music. The song blared through his ear buds his plan was working. He would embrace the melody and let the lyrics run through him. This was his chance to escape chaos and retreat to a familiar place of solitude.

The world around him began to slowly shift. He had once again reclaimed power over himself and his environment. He began to imagine the street lights dimming and in their place, stars emerged, shining upon him, as if to call him to place of higher power not that Nick believed in a higher power in the typical God sense, but he did believe that there might be something that we have not quite figured out just as yet.

As the music flowed through him, it invigorated him. It gave him life. It gave him power. But most of all, it gave him hope. Nick embraced the feeling and began to strog (to those unfamiliar with strogging, it is the act of strolling and jogging simultaneously. It is often done in a rhythmic fashion; but it should be noted that it is neither a performance nor a ritual, but rather, a felicitous walk to a specific melody).

The music had completely taken over, and Nick's mind had been able to transform his despair into something beautiful. After all, there is something beautiful about despair. It is through despair that we as people are able to empathize with others, thus, bringing us all closer together. It seemed to Nick that in that moment, he understood what it was like to lose something. This was not the first time that he had lost something he loved. He too had lost Ron all those years ago. However, it was the first time that he felt as though he had lost someone for whom he had true romantic feelings for.

It was not long when Nick was able to see his home – he was nearly there. Despite the fact that Nick was able to embrace his music and the environment, he could still hear the voice inside his head echoing. All this time, and it had not yet stopped. In fact, the closer he got to his home, the louder the voice seemed, and ignoring the repetitive sound was no longer an option. If being a hero made him Superman, then surely the voice inside his head was kryptonite. As the voice became louder, Nick's head began to throb. Nick screamed and wriggled with pain – he was losing control. The environment that he had created was disappearing and in its wake stood not reality, but a memory. Nick could see flashbacks of his accident. He saw his trip, the fall and the collision. The pain struck once more, and the environment changed again. This time, Nick was not viewing his origin story, but rather the after-effects. He saw himself, lying in a hospital bed, his sister by his bedside, holding his hand and weeping. While Nick knew none of this was real, and that this was simply his mind playing tricks on him, he could not help but feel that it was real, as if he was currently living through what he was seeing.

And then, it all went black.

17

THE STORY OF A SIDEKICK

The sun broke through the cracks in the window. In an instant, Nick's entire room was illuminated; and Nick saw darkness no more. Nick was in his bed, how he got there, he did not know. The last thing he could remember was seeing his home, the voice overpowering him, and his vision succumbing to the darkness. Yet, despite this horrid nightmare, he had woken up in his bed, as if nothing from the night before had actually happened.

Nick hurriedly sprung from his bed. He did not bother with his ritualistic morning routine. Instead, Nick opted to run downstairs and check to see if there were any signs that last night had even happened. Nick searched his home frantically, but alas, he could not find a single sign. Nick felt a sense of relief, after all, the night before if it had occurred was one of the worst nights of his life. So, if by some chance that he had in fact dreamt it all, well then, he might have a reason to be grateful.

118

A sense of comfort and stability began to flow through Nick once more. "I've gotten away with this one," Nick thought. A smile stretched across his face, his entire body feeling a sense of relaxation he had not felt since the accident. Things had worked out perfectly. And then he was struck with fear. A noise, although quite faint, was coming out of his pants pocket. Nick reached into his pocket slowly, as if handling the situation with the utmost care. There in his pocket laid his cell phone. Now, this may not seem unusual, but it was not the phone that struck Nick with fear – no, it was what was playing on it. Music could be heard coming through the speakers, and the song playing was none other than the Alicia Keys' track that had accompanied him on his terrible walk home.

Nick quietly turned the music off and plopped down on the sofa. He seemed to sink into it, as if he needed protection from the world around him. Perhaps he really did need protection. After all, he had just found out that his terrible, rotten nightmare was not a nightmare at all. He was not a hero at the peak of his powers, but a man, naked and bare. And so he sat, lost and without direction. "There must be a way to fix this – to make it all right again." And then it hit him. Despite his current predicament, he was not alone. Every hero had a sidekick and he had his. Nick quickly pulled out his phone, which for some reason continued to loop his songs from the night before, as if to once again remind him of his pain. Nick dialed Tom's number, and waited eagerly for his friend's response. The phone rang, but to no avail. Tom's voicemail kicked in, and Nick hung up. *"He might be busy, or sleeping. Either way, they were one and the same for Tom,"* he thought. Despite his disappointment in hearing the voicemail, Nick was determined not to let it get to him. He had already faced enough abandonment, and the thought that his friend would readily ignore him was not something he was ready to deal with.

Nick paced around as he waited for what he deemed a sufficient amount of time before calling again. He was sure that Tom simply missed the call, and that it would be very unlikely – even for Tom – that he would miss two calls. He counted to sixty very slowly and then called once more. He was sure that it would be plenty of time for Tom to realize that he had in fact missed a call and then standby for the follow-up. Nick began to count — one, two three... but then his mind raced. Every few seconds, Nick stopped and checked his watch — which was still not working, thus making the entire process redundant. Thirty-four, thirty five... Nick continued to pace, his breathing became heavy, and overall, he began to feel rather unpleasant. He did not want to think that he had lost Tom as a friend too, but yet he could not help himself from thinking so. He had no real reason to assume Tom had abandoned their friendship. One missed call was not grounds to even think such absurd thoughts. As Nick began to realize that his thoughts were both irrational and emotional — things that he both despised — it occurred to him that he had already counted far past sixty, and in fact, had counted to three hundred and ninety-four.

In one swift motion, Nick pulled out his phone and dialed Tom's number. The phone rang once more, and for a second, Nick had hope that Tom would pick up. Alas, all hope was lost immediately upon hearing Tom's now familiar answering machine. Nick tossed his phone carelessly on the sofa. In truth, he wanted to throw it against the wall, but he felt that breaking his phone was both impractical and illogical, regardless if the act made him feel better or not. Tom was not answering him, whether by choice or by sheer negligence, it did not matter. Nick began to pace once more, but upon viewing his phone against the sofa, he hurriedly picked it back up and placed it in his usual front-right pocket. Upon placing it into his pocket, Nick felt slightly more relaxed, as if structure and order could negate even the most terrible of feelings. Nick took a deep breath, closed his eyes and began to think. Tom was not answering his phone, but that did not mean that he did not want to talk to him. All it meant was that he was not answering his phone. So, logically, if one cannot reach another by phone then perhaps a face-to-face visit is in order. And so, that is how Nick decided that he was going to pay Tom a visit.

The walk to Tom's did not take very long, as Nick was far too preoccupied with trying to understand both the events of the present and the night before. His whole reasoning behind accepting the title of hero was to win Sam over. Well, that and the fact that admitting that everyone had made a mistake seemed terribly awkward and an overall nuisance, and Nick could not be bothered with any of it. After careful thought and consideration, Nick began to understand that he was not going to win Sam over and it was unlikely that she would change her mind, at least not anytime soon. It came to Nick that he needed a new quest. He had failed his previous quest to win Sam's heart, but if Nick learned anything from books and movies, a hero does not simply have one quest, but a myriad. He was far from ready to relinquish his heroic duties, so, it was only natural that he looked for new meaning behind the gift that he had been given. This optimistic approach was both strange and unusual for Nick, but Nick was not the Nick of old. No, he was a hero, and he was about to rally his sidekick.

He knocked on the door lightly three times. He still felt the idea of ringing a bell to be presumptuous. After all, a bell that calls another over was in his mind, both rude and archaic. Nick waited patiently. Well, as patient as Nick could be. However, once again, Nick was left waiting. Nick knocked on the door once more, but still, no one answered. It was then Nick decided to do something he hated. Nick opened the door and let himself in – a custom he was becoming all-too familiar with. As he entered the doorway, he was no sooner met with Tom himself.

There he stood, wearing nothing but an open robe and dingy-white boxers which matched perfectly with the greying of his once white walls. "Eh, what in the hell are doing? You just let yourself into someone else's home, do ya?" said Tom.

This caught Nick off-guard. He was sure that Tom would not mind him, or anyone for that matter, walking into his home. However, his previous conceptions had proven him wrong, as his dear friend was blasting him for his rather rude entry.

"I'm sorry, I called, and you didn't answer... I came over... because, I needed to talk. I had quite the horrible night, and, and I just want to figure it out. Actually, I thought you could help me figure it out. After all, you are my manager, or PR guy, or whatever it is that you do, I'm still not quite sure." Nick made his best attempt to smile politely, hoping that it would garner a similar response from his friend. However, his attempts to illicit some form of happiness failed miserably. If trying to make Tom happy was his second quest, he was now zero for two.

"You have the nerve... the audacity to come here after what you did last night!"

This too surprised Nick very much. However, he was not sure what surprised him more: the fact that Tom was clearly upset with him, or that Tom used the word audacity correctly. Either way, Nick was hurt, shocked, surprised, and felt various emotions that Nick did not particularly like.

"Forgive me, you have to understand that I have no idea what the hell you are even talking about?"

Tom let out a chuckle, and then turned around, as if unable to face his friend. Tom motioned numerous times with his hands, unable to speak with words, thus resorting to gestures. It was unclear to Nick what Tom was trying to say, however his frequent and jarring movements could only indicate anger and frustration. What he did to inflict this anger, Nick did not know. None of it mattered though, because Nick was beginning to realize his previous fears of Tom's abandonment were coming true.

"You are a real ingrate, you know that?" said Tom, his eyes widening and his hands continuing to make quick, erratic movements.

"What the hell did I do to you? Last night when I left you, you seemed perfectly fine."

"You stupid fool!" shouted Tom furiously. "That's just it. You left me. You were supposed to be my wingman. Those women were as good as ours, but no, you had to have a 'Nick' moment, and mess it all up."

All Nick could do was shake his head. Why he did it, he did not know. Perhaps he thought that repeated shaking would wake him up from his nightmare, or maybe he believed that continued denial of the situation would in fact negate the hostility all together. Either way, all Nick truly knew was that he was beyond hurt. He had lost his last friend. Nick lifted his wrist and stared at his watch, hoping that the magical comfort he had felt before could somehow work again. Alas, it did not. There was no way of ignoring this battle, he would have to stand strong.

"What... what the hell is a 'Nick' moment?'"

"Ya want to know what a 'Nick' moment is, huh? A 'Nick' moment is when someone takes a perfectly good opportunity and fucks it all up because the opportunity is 'different' than their usual sociopathic routine."

Now, it is never a wise decision to call another a sociopath under any circumstance, but it is even less ideal to do so during an argument. This was something that soon became clear to Tom who prior to this argument, had not had a real argument. That is to say, most of his arguments were one-sided, as he often spent most of his time ignoring others. It was his original plan to do the same with Nick, however, Nick's intrusion into his home forced his hand.

"I'm sorry. No, I really am. I'm sorry that my 'Nick' moment fucked up your chances to score with some floozy," argued Nick.

"And I'm sure that floozy you're interested in is so different. By the way, how did that go?" A sinister smile stretched across Tom's face. He had won his argument, he knew that.

Nick could not look at Tom, as tears began to well-up in his eyes. It was unlike Nick to cry   especially in front of others, but he could not help himself. There he stood alone, somewhere between heartbreak and the loss of a friendship. There was no Sam, and it was becoming increasingly clear that Tom was never really there either. Had Nick failed to notice Tom's selfishness, or had he chosen to ignore it?

"How... how can you be so cruel? I thought the party was for me. I thought it was my time to seize the things I want. And I thought... I thought you were there to support me... but... I guess I was wrong."

"You really are a stupid fool, Nick." And with those words, Tom walked up the stairs, leaving Nick alone in the hallway with his words.

Nick had lost more than a sidekick, he had lost a friend. While it is safe to say that Tom was not much of a friend, he was still there, and that was more than Nick ever asked for.

As he stepped out on to the front steps, he felt a cool breeze drift through. Nick bundled up his coat, crossed his arms, and with a sigh, began to walk home. *"What kind of hero am I?"* he thought, as he kicked a rocked against the curb. It was a fair question. Nick had no real quest, nor did he have any sense of purpose. And what is a hero if not purposeful?

He entered his duplex and took a seat on his sofa. He did not bother to take off his coat, instead opting to leave it on as a reminder of his fight with Tom. He did not speak, nor did he turn on his television. Instead, he just thought. Could his misfortune be some sort of karmic punishment for his lies and omissions? Or was it all just bad luck? Whatever the case, Nick was no longer flying, but falling, and he was not quite sure if he could ever recover.

18

THE STORY OF A FALLEN HERO

The sun broke through the cracks of Nick's window, and no sooner did his alarm begin to buzz. Nick grudgingly sat up as he rolled himself out of his bed. It was time for him to go to work, yet, all he could think about were the events of the weekend. A lot had changed since he had last gone to work. He no longer fantasized about Sam, as he knew full well that in no reality would they ever be together. And then there was the Tom situation. Yes, it was true that no one at his workplace knew who Tom was, or would have any idea that the pair had had a falling out, but he feared that he would be unable to hide it. Nick had a strange suspicion that his face would betray him. This thought was quite hard to literally swallow, and consequently Nick almost choked on his breakfast.

It was not all bad though. Since his accident, his workmates had treated him with much respect and admiration – and Nick had enjoyed that. As far as everyone knew, he was still a hero, and as such, he would expect only the highest of treatments. Nick was positive that despite the pain and loss he had suffered on the weekend, his workmates would surely more than make up for it.

Nick stepped out of his house and put on his ear buds, shuffling through his phone to find an appropriate song. After a short shuffle, Nick quickly settled on *When the Day Comes* by Nico & Vinz. And so began his usual stroll to work. His imagination wandered, as he looked to create a world of his liking. On this particular stroll, Nick did not see his usual picturesque atmosphere, but instead, he saw his rise to stardom from his lowly job in the IT department, to his accident, and finally to his heroic praise. And that is where it stopped. He could not for the life of him imagine what could come next. In his prior dreams he imagined Sam, and people cheering him through all his trials and tribulations. However, Sam was gone. Nick desperately hoped that his mind would find a way to find something amidst the confusion, but his dreams continued to end with his heroic praise. This bothered Nick tremendously, although he hated to admit it to himself. If his heroics only garnered praise, and no physical or social wealth, was there really a point?

Nick continued to stroll – albeit more lethargically – toward his place of work. Upon entering through the glass doors, he was taken aback by what came next – everyone was busy. Now, this may not seem surprising, as people are often busy at work, but what shocked Nick was the fact that not one single person noticed him enter. And as he walked through the lobby, turning his head and smiling at his fellow workmates, not one smiled or even looked back.

His stomach began to hurt, like when one forgets to eat for an extended period of time. "Did everyone already forget?" Only a few days ago, Nick had been lauded for his heroics as he walked down the halls. Now, just a few days later, no one seemed to remember, or even notice him. He could not let this happen. He had gotten a taste of celebrity, and there was no way he would be able to go back. After all, heroes cannot truly quit being heroes; it is in their blood.

"Hello," said Nick to a woman as she walked by.

The woman did not look up, but mumbled what Nick assumed was a form of greeting in his general direction. *Well, she seemed rude to begin with,* thought Nick.

"How are you today?" asked Nick to a man, as he walked parallel with him toward the stairs. The man stared at his newspaper, never once breaking focus. However, this man did reply with a very audible 'good', but that was where the conversation ended.

And then he saw her – Sam. She sat at her usual desk, flipping through her fashion magazines, or whatever it was that she was interested in this week. Nick stood still, staring at her. He did not fantasize, nor did he utter a sound, but just stared, thinking of what almost was. Just like the rest of his workmates, she too did not look up. After a few seconds, Nick could not bear to look at her anymore, instead opting to take his usual walk up to the second floor to begin his day.

His desk lay cluttered with various items and papers. He had neglected to keep it tidy since his newfound celebrity status, however, due to his recent predicaments, his untidiness came into focus. He could not leave it like this. His need for structure and order took hold as he began to reorganize his workplace.

For the next few hours, that was all he did – cleaning and organizing. It was not until he finished that he realized that he was alone in the IT department. Nick turned around and began to scan the room. He could not find anyone, and more importantly, he could not find Andy. Normally, Nick would be delighted to separate himself from his needy workmate. Yet, there, alone in the office, Nick felt a strange feeling. He quite missed having him around. While he did find Andy rather annoying, he also found him quite endearing – something that he had not realized until that moment.

As Nick pondered his feelings toward Andy, Kevin from legal walked by quite hurriedly.

"Excuse me," said Nick, as he called out to Kevin. Kevin stopped abruptly, and turned around. He was the first person all day to take notice of Nick's presence.

"Hey, what's up?" said Kevin, quite casually.

"Do you by any chance know where Andy is today?"

Kevin from legal paused for a moment, staring awkwardly at Nick, as if unsure of what he was even talking about. After a few moments of awkward silence, it became clear to Nick that Kevin had no idea who Andy was.

"Andy works in IT with me, he's a lanky fellow, glasses," said Nick, in his best attempt to describe his workmate.

"Oh, yeah, I thought his name was Nick."

"No, I'm Nick," replied Nick, rather annoyed that despite his heroics, no one seemed to actually know him.

"Oh, I thought you were Kevin."

This bothered Nick quite tremendously, as memories of his interactions with Sam began to flood his mind.

"No... you're Kevin, I'm Nick."

"Whoa, this is all blowing my mind. It's like everything I knew is wrong."

It was clear to Nick that no one in his office, or even building truly cared about him. No one seemed to even know his name. Beyond the scope of his heroics, it was clear to him that no one actually cared about him at all. That is, except for Andy. Andy was the one person who genuinely cared for Nick. And yet, Nick always pushed him away.

As Nick thought about this, he began to feel very morose. Was his entire life simply a self-destructive mess?

Nick removed his jacket from around him and dropped it on the chair behind. For a brief moment, the jacket seemed to float   like a cape in the wind. It was only then that Nick realized that he was not a hero, nor had he ever been one. Nick was just Nick: a lowly, average worker, in a very average city, in simply one part of the world. How could he ever think that he was special, that he deserved to be more than what was already given to him? As these thoughts swirled in his mind, he failed to recognize that Kevin was still standing before him.

"So, did you need something, Nick? Whoa, that still feels strange to say."

The dazed look upon Nick's face began to fade, as he slowly began to focus back toward what was in front of him. "I just wanted to know where Andy was."

"Ah, I heard he was sick or something. Not terminally or anything, just like a flu... which, by the way, is still very bad. I'm not trying to belittle his illness or anything."

The only words Nick managed to focus in on was the fact that Andy was sick. It was unlike Andy to be sick. Nick could plainly remember Andy coming in through various illnesses over the years. In fact, it was just last winter when Andy came into the office wearing sweats. Nick remembered this clearly, as he remembered thinking that Andy looked like a malnourished boxer.

"Is there anything else?"

"No," said Nick with a sincere smile. And with that, Kevin headed off, and Nick was once again alone in the office.

The entire room was quiet, and yet, Nick could not concentrate. He felt an angst from within, as if he knew that something was not quite right. As he sat upon his office chair, swiveling anxiously back and forth, he could not help but think about Andy being sick. *"He must be terribly ill,"* Nick thought. Nick stared at his computer screen, hoping to find a sign that might fix the problem. Alas, there was no sign, only a feeling. Not even the repeated shuffling of his solitaire cards could cheer him up.

And it was then that Nick decided to do two things he had never done before. One was to consciously place another's needs above his own, and the other was to pay Andy a visit.

19

THE STORY OF OTHERS

The walk to Andy's place was long and cold. Nick's hands began to freeze — with one hand holding a bowl of soup, while the other held directions to Andy's place. Normally, Nick hated writing directions, as he felt his memory was more than sufficient. However, because Nick had never actually been to Andy's and his decision to go was quite impulsive — at least to his standards — Nick was forced to walk around with a piece of paper detailing the most efficient route.

As Nick entered Andy's neighbourhood, he was struck with both fear and anxiety. Andy's neighbourhood was absolutely dreadful. The homes were small and rickety, and the people who walked the streets seemed angry and cold. Nick thought about putting on his headphones, but no music in the world could turn this picture into anything beautiful. Nick did not understand. Andy made roughly the same amount of money as him, so why did he chose to live in a neighbourhood like this? Nick was so frightened by his surroundings that he nearly walked right past Andy's home, which is a mucky townhouse that resembled more of a factory than a home.

Nick walked up the steps and knocked on what he presumed was once a white door. However, upon knocking, Nick was caught off guard by who answered. It was a beautiful, petite woman with auburn hair who appeared before him. Nick was in complete awe, and stood motionless with his mouth open. Not even the cold wind could sway his expression.

"I'm sorry," said Nick, finally finding words. "I must have the wrong house." Nick glanced at his piece of paper and then at the house number. Strangely, they seemed to match.

"Who were you looking for?" asked the woman. Her voice, if even possible, matched her beauty in the most felicitous way.

"Andy?"

"Yeah, Andy lives here. Wait, are you Nick?" said the woman excitedly. "Andy has told me so much about you. Please, come in." The woman hugged Nick who was not expecting such a warm welcome – though he did not complain.

Stepping in through the doorway, two small children – both girls – rushed past him. Nick immediately stopped, afraid that he might accidentally knock one of them over.

"Girls, please settle down, we have company," said the woman, gesturing Nick through a crammed hallway and into what looked to be there living room. "Andy, Nick is here."

"Nick?" Andy's voice bellowed from behind an arm-chair.

"Yes, Nick... from your work."

Andy immediately stood up, startled by the news of his guest.

"Nick, what are you doing here? I'm not complaining, I'm just... well, I'm surprised, to be honest."

The room was quite small, and it did not take many steps to move closer toward Andy, who stood awkwardly, fidgeting with his robe.

"I heard you were sick, and I thought I'd stop by," said Nick awkwardly. "Here, I brought you soup, although it is most likely cold. Sorry."

Andy stood perfectly still, only his glasses seemed to move as they began to slide off his face. Just as his glasses reached the tip of his nose, Andy quickly pushed them back up. "Don't apologize. That was really... nice of you. Please... please, have a seat," said Andy, as he began shuffling things around, clearing a path toward a large orange couch which was awfully tacky by Nick's standards.

"Thank you." Nick removed his jacket and took a seat. As he sat on the tacky couch, Nick tried desperately to make himself comfortable, but could not manage to do so. Now, it was not that the couch was uncomfortable, in fact it was quite comfy, despite how it looked, but it was Nick himself that was uncomfortable. For the life of him, he could not fully grasp the concept that he was visiting Andy.

"So, how are things?" Nick sat awkwardly, hunched over, too afraid to lean back and truly accept his surroundings.

"Other than the fact that I am sick and had to miss work, I'm actually well," chuckled Andy.

Nick made his best attempt to chuckle as well, but truthfully, he did not find it funny, and any attempt to over-chuckle might come across as insincere. And so, the two men sat silently, both fidgeting with their respective attire, afraid to make eye-contact and make the situation even more awkward.

Just as the situation began to evolve from awkward to strange, the beautiful woman Nick had seen earlier walked in holding a tray with cups and a teapot. "I come bearing gifts." The woman smiled and placed the teapot and the teacups on a rustic table between the two men. "This will help your cold, Andy, and Nick, this will warm you up. It's quite chilly out there."

"Oh, thank you. You're very sweet," said Andy.

The woman smiled, and then left the room Nick could still not take his eyes off of her.

"So, who is that? And who are those kids?" asked Nick, as he poured Andy and himself a cup of tea. "Is she a maid?"

Andy gave a very peculiar look, as if he was offended by the comment. It did not take much for Nick to take notice, realizing that he must have made a mistake with the women's identity. "I'm so sorry. Of course she isn't a maid," said Nick. "She's your sister, naturally."

Andy stared for a moment, and then let out a chuckle followed by a cough. As he regained composure, Andy looked up and smiled. "Nick, that's my wife and kids."

Few things truly surprised Nick. This was one of them. Nick nearly choked on his tea, upon realizing his mistake.

"That's your wife?" Nick swallowed another mouthful of tea.

"Yes."

"Andy, she's absolutely gorgeous. Why didn't you tell me about her, or that you had kids. I had no idea."

"I've invited you to dinner numerous times. I've even said, 'Clara wants to invite you to dinner.' Who did you think I was talking about?" said Andy, confused and a little annoyed that Nick had not paid any attention to his stories or his life.

"Andy, I am going to be perfectly honest with you, I thought Clara was your mother."

Andy sat silent, not an expression on his face. Nick mirrored this image, hoping that he had not offended him anymore by admitting that he thought Clara was his mother. However, just as Nick's fear of awkwardness began to rise, it quickly fell as Andy began to laugh heartedly.

"You thought she was my mother? Ha-ha-ha, honestly, Nick, you kill me. Normally I'd be insulted, but let's be honest, you've done and said far worse." Andy's voice boomed with laughter, a laughter so contagious, that Nick found himself laughing along. "You know, I always thought you never listened to my stories, but now I know you did, you just muddled them completely."

"Andy, I am really sorry, I had no idea you had a family," said Nick, as tears of laughter rolled down his cheeks. "On a side note, at least your kids took after Clara."

"Believe me, Nick, I am very grateful." A smile appeared across Andy's face as he said this. This was not a smile derived from humour, but rather, deep sincerity. Nick found the smile almost nostalgic, although he did not understand why he felt that way. Perhaps the smile reminded him of the way Kate smiled about her children, or maybe how she smiled about Ron.

Andy's laughter finally began to cease, and now it was simply a few chuckles. He smiled toward Nick, and Nick could not help but smile back. It was a strange feeling for Nick to enjoy someone's company — especially Andy's — so genuinely.

"So..." Andy searched for a new topic of discussion. "How's the hero thing going? You know, Clara and I clipped out all the news reports talking about you. We even made a scrapbook. I could show you... Actually, no. That would probably just embarrass you."

As the word hero entered the point of conversation, the entire atmosphere seemed to change. No longer was there a reason for laughter. To Nick, the only thing he could feel was pain and heartache. Andy seemed to notice, as his expression seemed to mirror that of Nick's, as if he was empathizing with Nick.

"Nick, what's the matter? You can tell me."

A lump began to form in Nick's throat, as he struggled to find words to express what exactly he was feeling. Nick glanced toward his watch — it was still not moving. He began to think about Ron, and how easily he could speak with him about things. However, since his death, he had not found another person he felt comfortable enough talking to beyond the banal conversations of the everyday. As he looked back toward Andy, who sat patiently waiting for him to speak, he began to realize that despite losing Ron, he always had Andy there. He may have been a fool toward Andy over the years, but now, when he needed someone the most, Andy was willing to listen — and sometimes, all you need is one person to listen.

"It's actually been quite dreadful."

"Nick, is everything okay?" asked Andy, leaning forward. As he did this, his robe opened up just enough for Nick to see things that no one but Andy's wife and maybe a doctor should ever see.

"Andy, your..." Nick pointed toward the opening in Andy's robe, however, Andy did not seem to get the hint. "Andy, your... your robe. It's open."

Andy looked down, but as he did, he opened his robe even wider, giving Nick an even greater view of the things that only Andy's wife and doctor should ever see.

"And now I can see everything. This is just wonderful," said Nick, turning his head up and to the left in order to avoid looking ahead.

"I'm sorry," chuckled Andy, crossing his legs and tightening up his robe. "You were saying it was dreadful?"

"You're a master of transitions." While Nick was slightly

disturbed, he could not help but chuckle to himself. "But yes, it's been horrible. All the attention, and then none of the attention. I pushed away my sister, and then I lost my friend. It's all just gone awry. I don't know what to even do anymore."

Staring blankly at a man, clearly distraught with his heart out, Andy sat wide-eyed and confused. He had never seen Nick so broken and vulnerable. Yet, here in his living room he sat, looking for something to help guide him back- back when things made sense.

"Nick, I can only imagine what you've been going through. I had no idea that things had taken a turn for the worse. Last I heard there was a party in your honour. When did all this happen?"

Nick stretched out his legs upon the sofa and placed his head against a pink cushion which he placed against the arm rest. And there he was, like a patient on a therapist's couch, divulging his heart to a man he once could not stand.

"I actually pushed my sister away shortly after the accident. I know she was just trying to look out for me, but it all scared me. I think she was scared that something would happen to me, because, well, something happened to Ron – her late husband. He died in a car crash, and ever since she has sort of clung on to me. I guess I pushed her away out of fear, a fear that I might hurt her the way that Ron's death hurt her."

Andy sat back on the couch and took in the words that had just been said before him. There was silence, but only for a moment, as Andy let out a long, "Hmmmmmmm," before speaking. "Nick, have you ever thought that by pushing your sister away, you're hurting her more; that the reason she clings to you, is because she needs you now more than ever?"

"I suppose... you're right. Andy, you're quite good at this. If IT doesn't work out, maybe you could be a shrink," said Nick, half-laughing.

It was the first compliment Nick had ever paid Andy, and Andy did not fail to take notice, as he sat up dignified and proud. While Andy's newfound pride was something Nick would normally make fun of, on this occasion he chose to ignore it, and let Andy have this moment.

"So…" said Andy, searching for another question or topic that the two could possibly discuss. "What else seems to be the problem?"

"Well, there's the whole Tom situation, but I'd rather not talk about that. I guess the big one is Sam."

"Oh, what happened with that? Did you guys talk? Oh, no you guys kissed? No, wait, you did more? High-five, Nick! High-five!" blurted Andy quite excitedly.

"Andy… no," said Nick, turning his head and shaking it in disapproval.

"I'm sorry, I got ahead of myself. Okay, so tell me what happened?"

"Basically, we went out, and I was really into her, but she seemed more interested in the idea of being with someone 'famous' than with me. And I also started hearing voices and blacked out on our date, and she left."

Andy's face looked askance, as he processed the fact that Nick had just claimed to blacking out and hearing voices. As he finally managed to comprehend the idea, regardless of how horrible and terrifying it actually was, his face regained normalcy.

"Alright, I'm not going to even try and get into the whole voices thing."

"Oh, I don't blame you."

"But the Sam stuff, I don't see how that is something to be down about," said Andy.

Nick sat up, as he leaned forward, unsure if he had in fact heard the words correctly. How could he not be devastated? The woman of his dreams did not want him. Of course Andy did not understand, his wife was nothing short of beautiful — he clearly had never faced such heartache.

"Let me get something straight. I had my heart broken by the woman I have been obsessed with, and yes, I will admit I was obsessed… since… since she started working with us."

Andy smiled coyly, his eyes first staring up and then finally returning toward Nick.

"You just said it."

It was clear by the confused expression upon his face that Nick did not understand. In fact, he did not want to understand. He wanted Andy to understand. Understand his pain, his loss, his, for lack of better words... shitty nightmare. Nick continued to gaze across the room, awaiting Andy's inevitable correction to his statement; but it never came. Instead, all that followed was truth, and all Nick could do was listen.

"You were obsessed. That isn't love, that isn't even like. Obsession is just lust, and nothing, and I mean nothing, will ever really come from that. When I think of Clara, and just to make sure, I am talking about my wife," said Andy, as both men chuckled over the previous misunderstanding. "When I think of Clara, I don't pine over her, and she doesn't pine over me. We simply ask for one another's company through... well, life. And that's what's great about it. Because we can ask for one another. We do not demand, and we do not expect."

Nick's heart raced as he replayed the words over and over again. *We do not demand, we do not expect.* He could not get it out of his mind. Had he expected Sam all this time? Perhaps not in the traditional sense, but he had expectations, that was for sure. It slowly became clear to Nick that he had expected Sam to be a certain way, for their feelings to develop the way he had envisioned it. But, just as Andy had said, he had never asked Sam about anything, he had barely even spoken to her. So why did he assume that it could be any other way?

The two men did not say anything, and yet, found solace in their mutual understanding. Nick picked up his cup and took another sip of his tea.

"Thank you, Andy. I really mean it," said Nick. "What's funny is, I think that while part of the reason for me accepting this whole hero thing was to win over Sam, I also think part of it was that I wanted to create a story. I wanted to create my story. I have often thought about why we do it. Why do we create and cling to stories? All this time I assumed it is because of our desperate need to escape reality. I, however, have learned this to be incorrect. We do not love stories to escape reality. We love stories because it gives us the power to feel, and boy did I ever feel." Nick let out a sigh as a tear broke free from his lashes and dripped down his face. With a single brush of his thumb the tear was gone. Andy did not say a word, but simply smiled, realizing that the moment was too important for words to interfere.

"Andy, can I ask you something?" Nick sat up straight and leaned forward. His tears were gone, and his voice had found words once more.

"Sure, anything."

"All these years, I've treated you terribly. Why have you always been so nice to me?"

Andy chuckled, as he lowered his head. "Uhh," he said, unsure of the right words to use. Andy lifted his head, as he ran his hands through his hair. "I guess..." he said. "You always looked like you could use a friend." Andy smiled, unsure of how Nick might take his response.

The corner of Nick's lips twitched as a grin formed across his face. "Thank you." His voice cracked, the words barely coherent. "Thank you for being my friend."

20

THE STORY OF STANDING TALL

The bitter wind cut through him like scissors through paper. After all that had happened and all that he felt, he would not let something as silly as weather deter him from his goal. Ever since his accident, he had neglected Kate but tonight, he would make up for that.

Nick trudged along the sidewalk, and with every step, he felt stronger, more determined. He thought of his sister, his niece, and his nephew, and he knew one thing: he loved them. Nick loved them, and yet, he could not remember a time when he had ever told them.

He could have just as easily called and told them, or called and asked for a ride, but Nick felt that he needed to do this. He needed to, of his own accord and by his own means, visit them.

It took him over forty-five minutes to reach Kate's home, but when he did, he felt a rush of excitement take hold. The last fifty meters or so, Nick sprinted with every bit of energy he had. The wind rushed past him, his eyes watered, and yet, he pushed on. As he stood at the foot of her door, he knocked riotously against the door.

"Hold on, hold on." He could hear the voice of his sister bellow from within.

The door swung open, and there she stood Kate.

"Nick?!" shouted Kate, as she looked upon her brother, shivering outside in the cold. Before she could tell him to come in and make himself comfortable, Nick threw his arms around his sister, tears rolling down his eyes. Kate's arms were left pointing up, unsure of whether her brother was hugging her or attacking her. After realizing that Nick was in fact hugging her, she let her arms hug him back.

"What's the matter?" Kate's eyes welled-up although she had no idea why. Perhaps it was simply the fact that she missed her brother, and here he was hugging her something that she knew he hated to do.

"I love you, and I am so sorry," said Nick, as he squeezed his sister tighter, lifting her in the air.

"I love you, too, but right now I can't breathe," said Kate, as Nick finally released his grip.

The siblings stared at one another for a moment, with a smile on each of their faces. As they did this, a rumbling of footsteps could be heard as both Anthony and Allison came storming through the hall.

"Uncle!" Allison and Anthony rushed Nick. Their tiny arms thrown against Nick's body from every angle.

"And I love you, and you," said Nick.

This caught both Allison and Andrew off guard, as they were used to their uncle being stand-offish. Nevertheless, their confusion did not deter Nick as he scooped them both in his arms, hugging and kissing his niece and nephew repeatedly.

"Uncle, are you on drugs?" asked Anthony.

"Anthony, that's inappropriate!" shouted Kate "But yes, that's a good question. Are you?"

Nick chuckled as he stood up to face his sister, his eyes still watering. "No, I'm not, and I'm not a hero either. I know I said I was, but there's so much that I need to explain, and I just feel like I need to be honest with you, because If you can't be honest with the people you care about, then who can you be honest with? The answer is no one. At least I think it's no one, honestly, I'm not even sure anymore. Oh, Kate, I've been a horrible brother."

"I have no idea what you just said," said Kate, as she stared at her brother. Although he stood perfectly still in front of her, Kate felt as if he was in pieces. "Nick, please slow down. What are you even talking about?"

"I'm not a hero. I lied."

Kate's brow furrowed, as she began to worry about the state of her brother. "Come in the living room and let's talk." Kate gestured Nick toward the living room and then turned toward her children, who were still standing beside their uncle, as if they were soldiers awaiting further instructions. "Children, could you give your uncle and me a few moments to talk?" Anthony and Allison nodded politely and scampered off.

Kate followed Nick into the living room, and each took a seat on adjacent couches.

"So, you were saying," said Kate.

"I was absolutely horrible to you." Nick's breathing quickened, and his eyes were swollen from the tears that poured out just a few moments ago. Though they had stopped now, even the slightest bit of emotion was sure to open the floodgates.

"You haven't been horrible, Nick. You have always been good to me," said Kate.

The words caused a pain in Nick's chest reminiscent of the night with Sam. Nick's hand clenched his chest for just a moment, before forcing his other hand to clasp it. There he sat, hand-in-hand, eyes swollen, and a pain in his chest that felt like an explosion.

"I haven't always been good to you, especially lately." The words seemed to stumble out of his mouth. "When this accident-hero thing occurred, I pushed you away. I was afraid, and I was wrong. And to make matters worse, I'm not even really a hero. I never meant to save that woman. I tripped."

"You tripped?"

"I tripped," said Nick. "My shoelaces came undone, and I ended up falling and knocking into her. I'm not a hero. And now, nothing I've done will matter. One day I will die, and I will fade into obscurity. And everything that has happened, everything I've done,

141

and will do will all simply be a distraction."

Kate reached out her hand and held Nick firmly, but gently. A sympathetic smile appeared on her face, and while it was beautiful, it was not overpowering. Her smile was a comforting one. Never boastful or insincere. "Oh, Nick." Kate's eyes began to water. "If everything in life is a distraction, then I choose to only be distracted by the most beautiful things. And I don't mean superficially either. I mean my children, Ron, music, a good book, and... you, my brother."

"I'm so happy to have found a way on that list, looks like I just made it," said Nick, half-laughing, half-crying.

Kate simply shook her head, as he tilted her head up to wipe a tear falling on her cheek. Finally, she let out a sigh, exhaling her emotions in an attempt to regain composure. She looked up to see Nick leaning forward, his hand in hers.

"I have news for you, Nick. You are a hero."

"I'm not sure if you understood what I just said. I tripped. I'm not a hero," Nick reiterated, a little annoyed that his sister was finding it hard to believe that his heroics were in fact a sham.

"Oh shut up," Kate said with a laugh. "You're not a hero because of that. You're a hero because of what you do every single day. What you do for me and the kids is nothing short of astounding."

Nick's brow crinkled trying to make sense of what his sister was telling him. He did not understand. What could he have possibly done for either of them? Over the years, he had been rude, quiet, anti-social, and yet, somehow, his sister found it all to be astounding. Perhaps she had used the wrong word, he thought. Kate had never been the wordsmith that he was.

"I haven't done anything."

"That's not true. You come twice a week to dinner, and sometimes more. You show up whenever I need you. And you've even watched the kids on days when I needed you   even though you hate kids. Sometimes, Nick, a hero isn't someone who does magnificent feats. Sometimes a hero is just someone who is there. It's the little things, Nick. The things you do every day. The things that you don't even think about that actually matter."

His chest clenched, but this was not the pain of earlier, but rather an overflow of emotions that he had been holding in for quite some time. As Nick exhaled, he half-choked in an attempt to prevent himself from crying. But then he looked into her eyes. Kate's eyes were no longer a dam, but a waterfall. And so he too wept.

"When Ron died, I didn't think I could do it. I had two small children and a low-income. I had no idea what I was going to do. Here were these two children who needed me, and all I wanted to do was cry because I had just lost the love of my life and the father of my children. Then you stepped up. I know you loved Ron, and I know it hurt you to lose him, and that's what makes it all so heroic. You helped take care of me, so I could take care of my children. And all this time, no one took care of you. Nick, if that's not a hero, then I don't know what is."

"I know... you... loved him." Nick's words jarred from his sporadic breaths.

"There is no 'loved', only love. I still love him, and I do it the best way I know how – simply."

Nick squeezed his sisters hand and placed his left hand on top of her other hand. And then he heard it – ticking. The watch had begun to move, and spin rapidly. Time was not moving normally, but it seemed as if everything was happening all at once.

"Niiiiick," called his sister. Hearing his name in that way had become an all too familiar phenomenon since his accident. But now, in this blur of reality and time, he knew now where it came from.

"Is none of this real? Has this all just been a dream?" Nick asked as the world around him began to swirl in a vortex.

"Did you feel?" The illusion that was his sister asked.

"Yes."

"Then it was real."

And then it all went black.

21

THE STORY OF HIM

Bright lights shone above him. All he could see was white. It took a minute or two for his eyes to readjust to his new surroundings. The room was quiet, all he could hear was the beeping of the heart-monitor next to him. Nick slowly raised his body, but it ached tremendously. "Ahhhh," moaned Nick, as he forced himself to sit upright.

There, awaking from a sleep in an armchair laid his sister. She rushed over to his side, her eyes watering from seeing her brother awake and about. "I am so glad, you're back." Kate hugged him tightly, her arms wrapped around his white and blue gown.

Nick winced as she squeezed tighter. Kate was afraid that perhaps letting go would in fact undo her brother's recovery, but what she did not realize was that her actions were causing Nick a considerable amount of pain. This realization hit her quite quickly as Nick finally let out an incoherent moan that resembled something a whale might make.

"I'm sorry, I'm just so glad to see you... awake." After careful thought, Kate finally removed her arms from around him. Kate rushed over and pulled the chair which she had been sleeping on closer, and then sat down.

"How long have I been out?" asked Nick.

The room was a mix of white and blue, but there was no mistaking where he laid. Nick glanced up at the heart-monitor which thankfully beeped at normal intervals. Nick stared at his hands, which were considerably bandaged. His body ached all over, he truly felt as if he had been hit by a car.

"It's been about a day, give or take a few hours."

"That's it?" Nick chuckled, but was immediately forced to stop as his sides were considerably bruised and bandaged. ".Judging by your tears, I thought it would have been weeks, or even months."

Kate smacked against his shoulder, forgetting that he had just been hit by a car. Nick winced once again — his way of reminding her. "I'm sorry, I forgot. I know that sounds stupid, but I've been a mess since I found out."

"It's okay, I understand." Nick gave a tight-lip, but endearing smile toward Kate, who reciprocated with one of her own.

"Oh, before I forget, the giant card with all the pictures is from your friend Andy," said Kate gesturing toward his bedside.

Nick looked at the table to his left. There, beside his bed laid a giant, tacky, god-awful card plastered with a giant picture of Andy and himself. Nick did not recognize the picture, as he knew for a fact that he had never posed with Andy before. Nick struggled as he reached for the card. Upon closer inspection, it became clear that Andy had photoshopped the two of them together. The picture showed Nick waving and smiling — two things Nick was sure he did not do. Normally, this would irritate Nick, but this time it did not. Nick opened the card, and within he found a picture of Andy and his family. Below the picture a message was written. It read.

Nick,

I am so sorry for what happened. I wish I had been there. It's my fault. From now on, I will pack two sandwiches, and I'll make sure they're both roast-beef on rye, just in case. Anyway, Clara, the kids, and I will be over again soon.

Wishing you a speedy recovery,
Andy

Nick closed the card and placed it back beside his bed. A smile stretched across his face as he let out a sigh.

"Andy seems like a good friend," said Kate.

"He is." This time there was no hesitation in his voice. He was not sure why he felt such a strange bond with Andy, but something about it felt real.

And then he remembered. The memories of his heroic-dream began to flood his mind. It was as if he lived two separate lives. A smile formed across his face, as he thought about the events that had unfolded. The good memories, the bad memories, it had all felt so real. And maybe it was real. *Who is to say what is real*, he thought. *All that matters is that you feel.*

"I want you to know, that I didn't mean to save her. I'm not a hero. Despite what the media or witnesses might say. I didn't intentionally save her. It was merely a fortunate accident," said Nick.

Kate kept her tight-lipped smile for a brief second before letting out a giggle.

"I am well aware of your serendipitous run-in. There were many witnesses at the accident, and well, they all saw you trip. Nonetheless, the woman you saved is still grateful. Actually, the flowers over there are from her." Kate gestured toward a bouquet of assorted flowers and a card propped against the vase on the nightstand.

"The woman is actually quite cute, and single I think. You should give her a call, hero."

"I don't know, maybe I will."

Nick glanced back toward the flowers and card. He was not entirely sure if he would call the woman, but it gave him comfort to know that he could if he chose to do so. Perhaps he would ask her to grab a cup of coffee, he thought. It might be a nice welcome back to the real world.

Nick looked back toward his sister, who was still leaning against his bedside.

"I want you to know, that I will always be there for you and your kids. And nothing will ever change that."

Kate grasped her brother's hand tightly, and he clasped hers back. The two sat in the hospital room, happy to have one another in their lives. And all fell silent.

The only sound that could be heard was the ticking of Nick's watch.

ABOUT C.A. JULAL

C.A. Julal grew up in the town of Whitby, Ontario. He received a Communication degree from the University of Ontario Institute of Technology and an Education degree from University of Toronto. You will often find him referencing *Lord of the Rings*, *Harry Potter*, and *Doctor Who* in casual conversations. Good tea and coffee are his kryptonite; but please never interrupt him during a Manchester United game.

ALSO BY C.A. JULAL

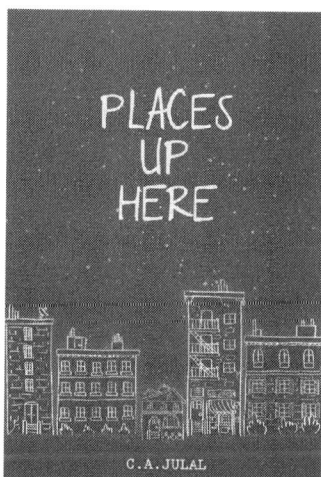

It starts at a train station. Infatuated with the idea of finding himself, the nameless protagonist leaves the comfort of the suburbs for the promise of a new start. Hidden within towering buildings is a quaint little house with a red door. This is where his first meets Sara, a petite young woman with brown hair, amber eyes, and a fiery attitude. Together, they take on the world – one fearless adventure at a time.

Praises for Places Up Here on amazon.ca:

"Never judge a book by it's cover, right? Well, I must admit the cover caught my attention immediately - but that's nothing compared to how locked I was to the pages inside. It was such an honest and yet simple tale of someone searching for meaning in life." - Samantha

"In this ultra-realistic look at the formative years of a socially isolated young man, the characters come to terms with their lives in non-formulaic ways. The protagonist's personal growth mirrors the growth in his writing as he learns how to navigate the world around him. Readers will find this to be a different take on the coming-of-age story." – Ava

Made in the USA
Charleston, SC
02 June 2016